SINISTER STITCHES

MARK CASSELL

Enjoy the Nightmare!

HERBS HOUSE

Published in Great Britain in 2015 by Herbs House
An independent publishers

1

For more about this author
please visit www.markcassell.co.uk

ISBN 978 0 9930601 2 0

Printed and bound for Herbs House

First Edition

For all those who are afraid of the dark

SINISTER STITCHES

A collection of short horror stories
in the Shadow Fabric mythos

CONTENTS

NEXT ON THE LIST

Through the reek of tobacco, stale sweat, and wet cabbage, the old man led Dan along the hallway. Shadows pressed in from either side where faded wallpaper curled—no portraits nor family photographs. The carpet crunched beneath each footfall. They entered a room with warped floorboards pushing into walls that bloomed damp patches.

"Please," the old man said from a throat filled with phlegm, "sit." He gestured at one of two threadbare armchairs that faced a tube TV.

A similar gloom to the hallway hung with the cobwebs, the dust, the emptiness. An afternoon sunlight attempted to infiltrate the yellow net curtains.

Meeting people like this made Dan hate his job. This was the next cottage on the list. The others had so far been surprisingly easy. He sank into the nearest chair, hugging his briefcase. A wooden ridge and too many springs dug into his arse.

"Sir," he said, "thanks for letting me in."

Either it was the armchair that creaked or it was the old man's bones as he settled into it. Sadness tugged his eyes, and his mouth slanted into jowls. "Call me Henry."

Straightening the briefcase on his lap, Dan flicked open the clasp. Its sharp crack echoed.

"It's a pleasure to speak with you, Henry." Dan straightened his back. "As I explained, I'm with the council."

"You did." He raised arthritic knuckles to a forehead that suggested a lifetime of frowning. "Something about the road."

"Yes, the proposed dual carriageway."

"I've been here a long time." The old man pressed the back of his hand against his forehead. The fingers twitched like a bloated, five-legged spider.

Dan nodded. "Sir—"

"I hate changes."

Something brushed Dan's neck. He shivered. It happened again, only this time up and into his scalp. A sharp pain and...

"Wha—" Dan jerked upright. The briefcase thumped the floor in a flutter of papers. Pens tittered across the floorboards. His heartbeat thrashed. A darkness washed over him and from every angle, colours squeezed inwards. His hands clamped the armrests. The old man seemed to shrink. The TV, the curtains, the damp patches, all diminished as the darkness churned.

Henry, slipping further away, still held the back of a hand against his forehead, those gnarled fingers curling, then extending, curling, extending...

Flashing colours, leaking darkness.

Nothing.

A dying sun pushed into Dan's vision. From an open door, wooden and aged, the burning rays poured down stone steps and across an earthen floor. He gasped, coughed, and struggled to move. Bound tight, rope dug into his wrists and ankles. The cold floor pushed through his clothes. Grit and grime covered his cheek, and a bitter taste filled his mouth. His cry stopped at taped-up lips, becoming a muffled grunt. Through flaring nostrils, his breath hissed rapid desperation.

Then he remembered: the old man, Henry, and the cottage.

Squinting up into the sunset, out through nettles and brambles, the old man's home squatted in the shadow of great oaks. What the hell? Why was he all the way out here? The rotted wooden panels surrounding him gave little away, and he guessed he was in a shed or outhouse. A sweet, almost tangy stink hung on the air, mixed with the heavy smell of earth and vegetation.

Managing to somehow calm his breathing, he twisted to look behind him.

Agony tore through his skull.

A miasma of colour again threatened darkness. Another cry, muted, snatched him back to the here, the now, to this insane situation. Panic snaked its way up from his stomach.

Something sticky tugged his hair as the pain subsided.

Henry, the old man, lay beside him, now shirtless to reveal a glistening paunch. Amid a haze of white chest hair, black slime clumped and oozed over pale skin. Leaves and mud and hooked brambles clung to his trousers. More slime smeared his bare feet.

But it was his hands that…what…? Whatever was happening with the old man's fingers challenged Dan's perception. Both hands dripped filth and just as before, they were clamped to his forehead. Yet those fingers were abnormally long. Still gnarly and twisted, but with smooth skin, stretched and taut. As were the forearms, they too were grotesquely misshapen and thin.

Slime flicked in all directions. It was as though Henry's pores oozed the stuff.

Dan moved again and a heat swept through him. That black filth was heaped between them. It pulsed as though with a heartbeat of its own. Some of the hardened lumps had fused with Dan's scalp, with his skull.

Agony drilled into his brain.

Henry rolled sideways, eyes hidden by those ridiculous hands. His mouth, slack, red, and dribbled slime.

One hand shot downwards and the fingers speared Dan's chest.

Hot pain tore through him.

Ribs splintered through shredding flesh. The bones cracked, snapped, and rose to meet, to *join*, those probing fingers. His heart wrenched in a rush of wet heat.

Snap-snap. Crack. Fusing and twisting.

And the darkness pressed in, just as Henry pressed closer. Closer.

Dust swirled in the final rays of a setting sun and the man returned the scattered papers to the briefcase. His spine popped but that was only this new shape settling. He lifted the case and sniffed; leather, relatively new. There was a hint of cinnamon...from where porridge oats...a son—Joe, four years old—had been careless during breakfast. His wife—Susan—had laughed. He had a well-paid job...the council...makes changes...he drove last year's BMW yet wanted an upgrade.

From the pocket of his suit, fitting snugly now his bones had fully shifted into place, he pulled out an ID tag.

Another name, another face.

He slid a finger across the plastic. Slime oozed beneath the fingernail, and he licked it. Bitter.

Dan Porter.

"I hate changes," he muttered and walked into the twilight, towards his BMW.

MIDNIGHT CLAY

As though the moonlight pushed him along, Owen freewheeled down the hill. The wind bit into his face, froze his knuckles. Often summer nights were like this, especially with a cloudless sky. If only he hadn't left his coat back at Jimmy's house.

A rumble in the distance, almost a howl, snatched his attention to the bend up ahead. He steered closer to the edge of the lane. He and Jimmy had an awesome evening; the new *Dungeons and Dragons* role-play game had stolen the day away. Before they'd realised it, night had fallen and Owen was late. Jimmy had beaten him with some lucky dice rolls.

The next game, Owen thought, would be war.

The rumble intensified; a vehicle approached at speed, still unseen. Perhaps a truck or lorry. Having cycled this route many times, he knew the lane was wide enough even if he did meet something that large. Still, he kept close to the grass verge.

Once more, his thoughts wandered to the game. Luck or not, next time he'd outsmart Jimmy.

Further ahead, along the winding road and through the trees, headlights forced back the darkness. Air-brakes hissed. A lorry, definitely, and it approached the bend without slowing.

Owen jammed on the brakes, the back wheel whirring on the tarmac.

He jerked to a halt.

The vehicle tore into the bend. Tyres screeched and juddered and groaned in protest. The trailer tilted, jack-knifed, and tipped. Something sleek, a silhouette against the night sky, leapt from the roof with what looked like enormous wings and too many limbs. Whatever it was, Owen had the fleetest glimpse as he threw himself sideways, dragging his bike. He rolled into the bushes, twigs and branches raked his hands and face. The lorry cleaved the tarmac, roaring like a metal dragon and uprooting trees and foliage, mud and earth.

His heart pounded in his throat.

After that there was silence, save for the creak of a buckled trailer wheel. And voices. Faint echoes on the wind from somewhere in the darkness. Not near the lorry but further away in the fields. Imagination surely; adrenaline from witnessing the crash. Imagination, too, had made him see that great...*creature*?

Entirely in his head.

He pushed himself up and staggered onto the road. The underside of the metal hulk loomed over him. A clump of mud and tangled brambles fell from the buckled wheel. Tiny glass beads covered the road, each one glinting moonlight.

If only he hadn't left his phone in his coat pocket, back at Jimmy's.

"Hello?" he called, heading for the cab.

No one answered.

He trod alongside the cracked headlights. Both were smashed, yet one remained blinding. Glass and plastic crunched beneath his feet.

There was nothing left of the windscreen; the cab roof crushed on the driver's side. It looked like a gaping vertical mouth without teeth. Above, the cab door was missing, allowing the moon to spotlight empty seats. No driver. He scanned the road from where it had come. Twisted metal, plastic, and glass scattered the tarmac.

The driver's body was nowhere in sight.

He circled the lorry as best he could given the density of the foliage, to scan a shallow ditch and the tractor grooves in the adjacent field. He ran a little way down the road, seeing whether the driver had been thrown from the cab before it hit the bend.

Again, nothing.

He trotted back to the cab. Careful not to snag his clothes, he climbed inside the glassless windscreen. Moonlight guided him without injury—jagged edges everywhere. The dashboard was a twisted mess. He rummaged only to find food wrappers and dog-eared fitness magazines. No phone, no way of contacting the police. Clambering out, he realised he had to get home and call the police from there.

Heading for his bike, he ran alongside the trailer. Wooden pallets, now vicious splinters, were cradled in metal cages between the wheels. He came round to the mangled rear doors and stopped. Crouching, he peered into the long length of gloom. At the far end, past chunks of masonry, several broken crates lay in the shadows. Knowing he should be cycling home, he stepped over the warped hinges and into the trailer.

It smelled of earth, of brick dust, and something sweet, something sickly. He headed for the crates, straddling busted pallets and rubble. He reached the nearest crate and read the label: *Handle With Care*. Straw poked between cracked panels. He slid his fingers beneath a wooden board and tugged. The snap-crack echoed. Removing another, he peeked inside. A dozen or so black stones about as large as his fist huddled among the straw like eggs in a nest. Leaning with one leg off the ground, he reached in. Damp straw poked his fingers and he grabbed one of the stones—cold and heavy.

He lifted it out.

Just enough moonlight pushed into the trailer for him to see. Mostly smooth, a kind of marble effect streaked through the stone; a kaleidoscope of colour blended with that deep, dark black. Bringing it closer to his face, he—

A thump rang through the trailer. From overhead.

He grabbed the edge of the crate. A splinter tore his palm but he hardly felt it as he looked up.

Another two thumps followed in quick succession.

He shoved the stone into a pocket and ran, leaping over the debris. He stumbled into the fresh air, turned and looked up. Dangling over the side near a missing wheel, a denim-clad leg twitched. An arm, too, flopped over the side. Blood dripped from the fingers.

Owen froze. That hadn't been there a moment ago.

Someone stood over the body. The person was tall, broad shouldered and wore what looked like a priest's cassock under flowing robes. Peculiar markings covered the robes, reflecting moonlight as though every symbol and glyph was stitched in silver. He held a staff or perhaps even a spear. His bald head glistened on a thick neck. Owen couldn't see his face. The man cocked his head as though sensing him and raised the spear…and rammed it into the driver's chest. Once, twice. Then a third time. Blood misted the air.

The man turned.

He had no face. This was no man. He—*it*—had only a blank head, like a white balloon, smooth and featureless. No, not entirely featureless; where each eye should be was a row of uneven stitches.

The ground seemed to suck at Owen's feet. Silently, he screamed at them to move, to get him out of there, but he could…not…move. He had to grab his bike, cycle away, get away from there. Now.

"Child," a low voice blasted into his brain.

"Wha—" His throat tightened. He looked around. "Who?"

Inside his head, the voice bellowed, "You were in the wrong place at the wrong time."

The blank-faced creature gripped the spear with both hands and leaned on it. Those stitched eyes somehow bored into Owen's mind. That, Owen guessed, was precisely what was happening. How else was it speaking to him? The thing didn't have any lips!

Churning shadows looped around the creature's torso, toying with the robes and tracing along the sigils and glyphs. Framed by fading moonlight, the creature reached down with an impossibly long arm and grabbed the driver's ankle, then hurled the body over the edge. Dead limbs cartwheeled almost comically and slapped the tarmac, spattering blood. The chest was cleaved open in a bloody mess of jagged ribs and a shredded jacket.

The creature leapt from the roof, its robes and cassock billowing, spear held high. Wispy shadows trailed behind. More floating than falling, it landed beside the body.

Owen pressed himself into the bushes and stared, craning his neck—this thing had to be at least eight-feet tall.

Its voice heavy like a shovel dragged across concrete thundered in his head. "Stop referring to me as creature. Lesser-beings like you mortals are creatures. *Demon* is more accurate. I am more man than mankind was ever intended to be."

A lump filled Owen's throat.

"You," said the demon, "should not have interfered."

He couldn't look away from the demon's stitched eyelids. Absurdly, all he thought of was the *Dungeons and Dragons* game he'd played earlier. It was as though he stood face to face with one of the characters.

"Interesting thoughts, child." Tilting his head, the demon leaned forward. "You have met my kind before."

He most certainly had not. Tabletop role play was one thing, but this?

"You know of magic, of spellcasting. Of witchcraft." The demon leaned closer still. "And you have defeated demons."

Owen's heart thumped in his head, louder almost than the demon's words. He gripped the stone in his pocket.

"Interesting," the demon said again.

He had to get the hell away from this thing. Now. But his legs wouldn't listen. Although his bike was fairly close, it felt miles away.

"You have something that belongs to me." This demon, this man, reached out, fingers curled upwards. "Give it to me."

With a shaking hand, Owen lifted out the stone. It seemed much heavier, warmer.

The demon snatched it. "You should have ignored my interception and continued on your way."

"But—"

"A war is coming, child. A war between worlds, between darkness and an even-greater darkness." The demon drummed his fingernails over the stone. Tick-tick, tick. Ticktickdick. The stone glowed with an inner light, a red tinge deep within the blackness. "None of this should concern you. However..."

A darkness smothered the demon's head, spiralling like smoke. Faint tendrils of shadow coiled around the stitches that wove through his skin. Behind his head, behind that glistening dome of mottled flesh, moonlight darkened. The demon straightened his back, robes and cassock swaying. He let go of the spear and it balanced vertically on its tip, defying gravity. Still with those stitched eyes fixed on Owen, he wrenched aside the robes and pressed fingers against the folds. The digits lengthened and sank into the fabric, disappearing into a liquid darkness. The way it played with light bent Owen's perception. Where he looked, light did not belong there, *could not* belong, yet a shimmering haze of shadows somehow allowed him to watch the demon's fingers twist into the darkness and disappear up to the knuckles.

Giddy, his knees buckled and he fell to the ground, half on the grass verge, half on the tarmac. It was as though his entire body had given up—all he could do was watch. And he knew this was precisely what the demon intended.

Owen. Must. Observe.

White energy trickled along the demon's robes and sparked around the glyphs and sigils. He removed his fingers and black slime stretched and drooped. Dark, stringy.

"I mould this clay…" That voice reverberated inside Owen's head. "…With Darkness in mind."

Kneeling as if to pray, the demon held out his arms. In one hand, he clutched the stone, and in the other, he cupped the dripping slime. Pressing them together, the two substances moulded like clay. The darkness and red streaks merged, sparking with an inner fire. Faint, yet fierce. Still kneeling, he extended his arm to drag the clay across the tarmac. As before, his arm lengthened, poking from beneath gaping sleeves, muscles flexing, stretching and reaching. He rubbed it across the tarmac, left and right, swift movements, faster and faster, becoming a stuttering blur.

Owen could not keep up with those frantic movements. It was as though he watched from much further away, like he saw all this through the eyes of someone else.

A black rectangle formed over the tarmac, but it had depth like a pit. Deep, dark. A black hole, no less, containing a bubbling impenetrable darkness. Again, it messed with Owen's perception; it hurt to look at and all he wanted to do was look away—but no chance. He had to observe. He must obey.

The demon stopped and leaned back, those stitched eyes raised to the faint moon overhead.

Like heavy smoke, the shadows now obscured the trees, the trailer, the debris. It was only Owen and the demon, and the driver's bloodied body, surrounded by the cloying darkness.

In similar swift and stuttering movements as before, the

demon grabbed the driver's body and pressed it into the black hole. The arms and legs flopped into the writhing darkness and it floated on the surface that now bubbled and rippled like dark water. Denim and cotton smouldered, wisps of smoke twisting upwards. Skin tore and bones cracked, churning together with soggy clothes and that liquid darkness. The demon dipped a fist into the mix and stirred. Muscles rippled along his forearm as that limb stretched impossibly long. Making circular movements, round and round, juddering and stuttering, the demon stirred. Clay and flesh, shadow and bone crackled and melded together.

Stirring, churning, the demon jerked and shuddered, wrapped in a kind of ecstasy. His head back, stitched eyes still on the moon.

Red and black mixed and bubbled.

Churning and stirring…

After the longest seconds of his life passed, Owen watched equally horrified and fascinated—frustrated and fearful that he could not move—as finally the demon stopped. His arm shrank back to its usual length. Now burying both arms into the disgusting mix, he yanked out a wriggling sheet of fabric. Dark, bloody chunks of flesh now stitched with the shadows, knitted together like a patchwork blanket. It dripped and hissed on the tarmac as he laid it aside. Strips of coloured cotton and denim were linked, woven with jagged sections of skin that pulsed and seethed as though the entire thing breathed. And it did breathe. Owen had no doubt that was precisely what this fabric was doing; pulsing, throbbing, living and breathing.

Somewhere far at the back of his mind, he knew he should now be escaping, pedalling fast…but there was something keeping him there. He had to stay, to run would be foolish. Such an opportunity; this demon will reveal so much more. There were unspoken promises. This demon would show him everything. Everything.

He had to run. Now.

But no. He would not. *Could* not.

Owen was almost ready to embrace what he was there for.

The shadows retreated to reveal the underside of the trailer again. Multicolour streaks played in the fading darkness as though a TV screen flickered, colours mixing with the shadows.

Apparently oblivious to the shifting atmosphere, the demon continued to stitch shadow and skin, creating another grotesque piece of fabric.

The dirty shades of colour opened up and became the silhouette of someone, or something. Another demon? But this image was different, almost elegant; smaller, frail. The blurry form of what Owen could only describe as an old hag appeared. Her hair was grey and fine, yet her face was hidden in a twist of darkness like a black whirlpool. She extended an arm. Her fingers smouldered as they reached through the shadows and into the world. She caressed the top layer of fabric.

Owen understood. He knew this was a witch, some phantom from history when witchcraft was dark and dangerous. She was on the 'other side', dipping an arm into this world, *his* world, to claim that grotesque rectangle of flesh and shadow. Any witch that needed such a horrific thing surely would not be a white witch. None of this was white magic.

"You, child," the demon's voice echoed in Owen's head, "certainly appear to have knowledge."

The hag pulled at the fabric and it slurped off the ground. She whipped it up over her shoulders and wore it like a shawl. She stroked it with gnarled fingers, her face remaining in a hurricane of coiling darkness, and finally retreated into the shadows. Again the darkness swirled and more forms shifted. One at a time as the demon laid out more of these garments, a dozen more women approached. Some old and frail, some young and slender, shimmered in the darkness, little more than haunting silhouettes and not once revealing their faces. Each flowed with the haze of shadows to claim their shawls, only to retreat and to make way for another, and another.

A small voice, freaking out somewhere deep within him, screamed and screamed at Owen. Runrunrunrunrunrunrunrun! That voice, fainter and fainter, a hollow echo of reasoning, of reality, shrank into a darkness that he physically felt clog his mind. Lower and lower Owen slumped, now huddled almost foetal-like on the edge of the road.

Each shawl slipped through, dribbling blood and blackness, sucked into another world.

The remains of the driver's body had by now blistered in a mess of black and crimson. The demon prodded it with his fist and hooked out a clump of blood-soaked clothes streaked with black goo. He dropped it. With a slap and a splash, dark blobs flicked across the tarmac and spattered the demon's face. Droplets collected around his stitched eyelids and ran down his veiny cheeks like tears.

Eager witches hovered at the threshold of the portal.

In one flash of motion, the demon snatched up the last garment, just before another arm from the shadows took it. "Wait, witch!"

The arm vanished into the roiling shadows.

Holding the shawl out, the demon stepped towards Owen. The cassock rasped over the tarmac, swaying. Those glyphs sparked, charged a fiery red and white. In his hands, the shawl seethed and wriggled and curled at the ends. The same energy trickled along the stitches, weaving along the seams.

"You," the demon said, "will now serve me."

Owen lowered his head.

"My midnight companion," the demon added, "my clay is yours."

The shawl hugged Owen's shoulders as the demon let go. Where it touched his neck, his spine tingled and warmed. Something like electricity rushed through him, outwards along his legs and into his toes, along his arms and into his fingers, up and into his brain. Every nerve charged and powerful, energised. Ready.

He was ready.

The demon stepped back. Blood and darkness dripped from his fingers. It hissed as it pooled the tarmac, soaking the hem of his cassock.

The blackness—so warm, so welcome—swelled inside Owen's mind. He would obey the demon, his master. Together, they would find more flesh to clothe the phantom army, the troops that lay in wait on the other side, awaiting the coming war.

A DEMON'S THREAD

"Demons tell campfire stories, too." – Anonymous

1.   *Occultus*

When a photographer falls he's going to protect his camera, and when gravity snatches my clumsy arse that's precisely what I do. Birdshit and moss, tiles and rotted wood fall with me. The jagged shape of daylight shrinks. I hug my camera and plunge into the darkness, and…

Pain explodes.

My lungs burn and my vision morphs into lightning flashes that betray the black void. I squirm, cradling my SLR. I try to breathe but the agony rages. I clench my teeth as air rattles my lungs and I taste a metallic stickiness. My legs, my arms; I feel them, thankfully. The pain subsides, marginally, so I guess I'm okay.

With a free hand, I reach out to claw wooden boards, dragging grit and filth. I sit up and squint into this nothingness. The stink of damp, of cold stone and decay, strangles me. I cough and pain stabs me in the chest.

Something moves nearby; a wet sound, a slurp like something dislodging.

Silence squeezes me. Had I actually heard it?

The SLR lurches in my hand. A clamminess brushes my arm and grips the camera. I pull it closer, muscles straining.

It's wrenched away in a spray of slime.

"Hey!" I shout. Somehow the darkness swallows the word.

More slurping, wet and heavy.

I shuffle backwards and kick out. My flailing arms slap the

curved brickwork. No exit. Mortar scratches my skin. No. Exit.
The cold wall presses against my spine.

The darkness thickens, tightens.

My heart crashes against my ribcage, stealing the silence.

The camera's flash pulses for a moment, and an oval
whiteness fills my vision; a face, blank, featureless with only dark
veins beneath glistening skin. The flash goes off fully, lighting
the surrounding brickwork and that faceless monstrosity
attached to a bulbous sweaty body, squat and seething atop
splintered floorboards.

The bare, curved walls—no exit!—prevent any further
retreat. I claw at the filth I sit in.

Black. Cold.

Again, that wet shuffling sound. Something flops. More
slurping as before, yet this time frantic. Eager perhaps?

Silence, once again. Just my heartbeat punching the seconds
that pass…

2.   *Evil Inside*

I have no happy memories of her when I was a little girl. The
woman broke my doll. That had been, what, thirty years ago?
She wasn't even a relative—just one of those people you
referred to as "Aunty" out of respect. That sweaty chin, her
jowls swaying as she bent down, insisting on a kiss…only ever in
front of Mum. Once we were alone, she had a bear-like grip. I'd
be dragged, thrown to the floor, always bullied by a glance; a
spear of blatant irritation. Her voice, like a shovel dragged over
gravel, and that heavy stink of body odour, cabbage, damp.
Breath like something rotten.

I resent my mum for always leaving me with that woman,
and perhaps you could also blame her for what happened last
week. What's that? Yes, I suppose this is a confession. Aunty
broke my doll, I told you.

The crunch of her bones wasn't as loud as the crack of my
doll's head as it smacked the kitchen floor all those years ago.

Aunty still has the same floor, funny enough. Yes, I still call her "Aunty", even now. And her head didn't bounce like my doll's did. I remember the way those little plastic eyes broke loose and shot inside the head, the rattle as they settled, the darkness within. Black like Aunty's soul.

Of course, I had to do the same to Aunty's eyes. When my thumbs pushed into her sockets, that wetness oozing, popping, there wasn't any darkness there. Even if, as I truly believe, her soul is black, there was nothing to suggest the evil inside her. I guess you could say I'm disappointed. There was a gooey redness. So much, it spurted. No black. Just red.

Oh look, I think there's still some under my fingernails.

3.   *Of Earth and Fire*

The shrooms glisten in the afternoon sun, bulging from the wheelbarrow. I stand back and wipe dark streaks down my overalls. That cloying stink thickens in my lungs like the time I'd discovered a dead fox beneath the shed, maggots seething, all rot and grey meat. These shrooms are like that; grey and black, festering, pulsing. Who'd ever seen such a thing?

Indoors to clean up. There's TV to watch and a meal to be had. Shepherd's pie. Much later, I've a toothbrush in my gob as noises, a roar and crackling, yank me to the bathroom window: a blinding light, white and yellow, in the garden. The wheelbarrow's on fire. What on Earth?

My bare feet pound the stairs two at a time.

The backdoor swings wide and crashes against the wall. Kitchen shelves rattle. I lurch into the garden, the cold paving biting my feet. I grip my toothbrush and squint into the blazing wheelbarrow; those bloody shrooms.

My eyes dart around. Where's the hosepipe? There, coiled like a snake beside the tomato plants. But my feet fail me, root me to the ground.

This strange fire rages.

Helpless.

In the flames, the burning mass shifts. Not the shrooms, something else. Toying with my vision to create shadowy phantoms. Churning within the fire...is a face? Black and narrow eyes, a sharp nose, and mouth wide with needle teeth. Squirming, teasing. First it's there, then it's not.

My feet twitch and I shuffle forward. I don't mean to. I don't *want* to. My head is heavy and a presence of...of what—evil?—leaks into my periphery, clamps my mind. Another step closer, closer to the blazing wheelbarrow. Smoke slides down my throat. I cough. Heat prickles my skin.

And still I walk.

Tendrils of fire reach for me, just as I reach it. The plastic of the toothbrush melts in my hand. Agony roars. I slip, arse down on the dew-soaked grass. The fire wraps around my hand, my wrist. Up my arm. Lancing pain, yet strangely detached. Like the pain is someone else's. The patchy shadows twist with the flames to embrace me. Warm, soothing. The darkness bleeds as the fire bursts around me. I crawl, slither and reach across blackened grass. My flesh is no more. I clutch with burning fingers, yet I have no hands.

Body, nothing more than fire. As liquid flame, I reach the garden perimeter. Fire crackles as I spread outwards. I slip between foliage, scale the fence, up and over, burning, and out into the street, reaching for Mankind beyond...

Once again, here on Earth.

I am.

Fire.

"And his eyes have all the seeming of a demon's that is dreaming."
– Edgar Allan Poe, *The Raven* (1845)

ON THE VINE

Shane's legs tangled with his sleeping bag. He fumbled for a torch, snatched it, and almost dropped it. Again something thumped outside the tent, scratching the canvas. He sat upright and thumbed the switch. Light speared the darkness. He squinted at the apex in the tent roof.

Something pressed against the fabric...and a barbed vine pierced through. Its end hooked like a beckoning finger. The thing tore downwards—so many barbs—and the canvas, frayed and jagged, flapped with the wind.

He grunted and kicked away his bedding.

The vine twisted like it had purpose, reaching for him. Cold air and the stink of something rotten poured in. He choked.

"Carla!" He shook his wife in the sleeping bag beside him. "Wake up!"

He scrambled onto his knees.

"Carla!" He coughed. The smell reached into his lungs.

The vine lashed his face. Grimacing, spitting agony, he flailed with both arms. Barbs sliced his forearms and the torch flew from his hand. It smacked the groundsheet beside Carla's head, spotlighting her closed eyelids, and flickered once...twice...and blinked out.

Darkness.

Feeling the most naked he'd ever been, despite wearing shorts, he backed into a corner. The damp fabric clung to his back. One hand swiped at the vine and barbs lacerated his flesh. His other hand fumbled for the lantern he knew to be somewhere near. Miraculously, he found it and prodded the *on* button.

Light exploded. He winced, blinded by both glare and pain.

The vine—more a *trunk*—recoiled like a cobra, framed by torn canvas and black night.

"Carla?" How could she sleep through this?

With awkward hands slick with sweat and blood and fear, he grabbed their food bag. Knife. He needed a knife. He looked down and...

The trunk smashed into the back of his head. The barbs raked his scalp. Darkness stole his vision, for only a second, and he swayed. Reflected in the serrated blade he held, the lantern banished his threatening darkness. Before he and Carla had left for this camping trip, she had teased him and said they'd not need a bread knife, it wasn't for camping, they'd not use it.

He felt his blood rushing through him, roaring in his ears and also dripping from his arms and head. His breath short, sharp in his lungs. Again, he choked.

The trunk lashed at him. He clutched it—the damn thing had *grown*—and the barbs lanced his palm. Lightning pain tore up his arm. As he gripped, digging in fingernails, he brought up the knife and hacked. The blade sliced through the trunk in a spray of dark filth. It spattered his face, stung his eyes, and dribbled into his mouth. Bitter, foul.

Carla screamed.

"Get out of here," he shouted at her. "Now!"

The trunk wrenched from his grip, the barbs further shredding his skin. Black gunk peppered the walls.

Carla's sleeping bag had shifted to reveal the torn groundsheet. Grass and earth bulged, and coils of smaller vines had twisted into her bedding. The zipper was mangled, perhaps even melted. She thrashed, still screaming. It rattled his brain. The sleeping bag bunched and slid down her body, now covering only her legs.

Shane gasped.

Where her night-shirt, the blue one with daisies on it, had ridden up, the flesh across her navel glistened; mottled and covered in pustules. Several oozed. Beneath her, half-buried in the disturbed earth and half-protruding from her skin, smaller vines wriggled like grass snakes. She twisted left and right, and uprooted those vines. The earth seethed as more vines erupted, seeking out her skin once again, each extending and whipping.

The sleeping bag slipped further…

Cold air hissed through Shane's clenched teeth.

Downwards from Carla's hips was the barbed trunk. No legs. Seamlessly that bastard trunk blended with her mottled flesh and burrowed into the ground. As she writhed to and fro, so too did the trunk overhead, raining black goo.

Shane fell back. The knife slid from numb, bleeding fingers.

His wife's eyes were still closed and she reached out with pale arms. The lower half of her body, the vine trunk, yanked the tent fabric. More filth sprayed and spattered his face. He blinked away that stinging muck.

Poles snapped in a tangle of canvas. The tent collapsed.

Carla wrapped the trunk around him, coiling. Tighter, ever-tighter. The barbs tore into his flesh. He yelled and grunted, wrestling. Useless.

A rib cracked. Then another.

Still she screamed. And Shane joined her.

THE ARTIST AND THE CRONE

I guess there will always be something in Mabley Holt to keep me here. Even after all the crazy stuff back in the spring, I returned and bought this tiny cottage with its equally tiny garden hemmed in by a precarious ragstone wall. As a man of little needs this was a perfect place to settle.

Perhaps it was stupid to think things wouldn't catch me up.

My one neighbour whose cottage was marginally larger than my own was a young lady of a similar age to me, with a reserved smile. If I thought my garden needed attention—those nettles were tall enough to sting your face—hers was equally neglected. We'd acknowledged each other when I'd moved in and that had been it.

After three weeks and kind of settled in, I dozed in front of a late night TV programme. A scream jerked me upright. On my feet, I staggered. That shrill cry still echoed, if not through the house but through my head. I yanked open the front door and stepped into the night. A cold moon pushed down on me just as the cold paving pressed up into the soles of my feet. I ran towards my neighbour's house. The place was silent and dark.

She'd had a nightmare, that was all. I headed back inside to bed.

Morning came and I awoke to the sound of thumps and clatters as though someone threw things in temper. I leapt from bed and raked fingers through my hair. Pulling aside the curtains without thought of my nakedness, I glared out the window and into her garden.

Dressed in a paint-spattered jumper and jeans, my neighbour stood beside a wheelie-bin. Its lid was up and rested against the ivy-shrouded fence. She was upending a number of shoeboxes and cartons, pouring out paint bottles and brushes and all manner of art supplies. Swiping away her dishevelled hair, she stepped backwards and looked up.

At me.

I twisted sideways, suddenly realising how naked I was, and the edge of the dresser stabbed my spine. She must've seen me. I waited, my back pressed to the cold wood. By the time I leaned sideways and peaked around the curtains, her garden was empty. She hadn't even put the bin lid down.

The day came and went; a day that I spent reading. Recently, I'd been reading a lot. All the books I'd inherited, books that truly belonged in a museum, were a mine of information that I hoped would help me understand a little piece of my troubled past. I'd even thumbed through a few books relating to local witch trials—it seemed Mabley Holt hadn't escaped witchcraft back in the 17th century, and given the small dealings I previously had with a magic that was most definitely black, that came as no surprise. The Shadow Fabric, a sentient darkness, was perhaps the most blackest of the arts imaginable.

Having just finished dinner, I heard my neighbour scream again. Only this time much closer, from outside perhaps. I took the stairs two at a time and ran into my bedroom, to the window. She stood in her garden, her face illuminated by the roaring flames from a twisted, shrunken bin. Thick smoke corkscrewed upwards.

Back downstairs again, I snatched my boots and yanked them on. One was bulkier now I'd modified it to conceal a weapon—these days I was always prepared. Keeping the Witchblade to hand was comforting, and as far as I could tell it was the only one in existence. I yanked open the back gate and ran alongside her house, over cracked paving and brambles threatening to trip me. The crackle of flames was louder as I approached. I stumbled into her garden. The stink of plastic and chemicals stung my nostrils.

Dressed in the same paint-splashed jumper as when I'd seen her that morning, she threw me a glance then looked back at the fire. Flames roared. Spirals of grey-black smoke reached the twilight clouds.

She scanned her garden. I guessed she looked for something to put out the fire. If we could contain it fast enough we'd not need the fire brigade. I ran over to where a hose coiled, tangled with grass.

"This attached to anything?" I shouted.

She nodded, hair catching in her mouth. She hooked it out.

"Turn it on!"

She seemed doubtful for a moment. I dragged the hose closer to the flames as she vanished round the corner. Heat prickled my face. The hose jerked, spat, then hissed a stream of water and I directed the nozzle around the edge of the inferno. Smoke belched and I cupped a hand over my mouth and nose. Waving the hose left and right, I doused the flames and gradually worked inwards. Defiant at first, the fire diminished.

Eventually, I stood back but kept the hose aimed at the dirty rainbow of molten colours. Several fence panels showed a few scorch marks. The ivy had burnt away and water dripped from the shrivelled and blackened ends.

"Reckon you can turn it off now," I said.

Her face, although relieved, seemed to shrink. Her mouth slightly open, she disappeared round the corner again. I heard a couple of squeaks and finally the flow dribbled. She returned just as the last drip splashed my boot.

"I'm Leo," I said.

"Pippa," she whispered, "and thank you."

I coiled the hose in a pathetic attempt at neatness, and dropped it on a rusted garden chair. My cuff had ridden halfway up my forearm and something made me quickly tug it down to hide the mark, the scar—I've called it a scar all along but I've always known it was more than that.

For something to say, I said, "Guess you're an artist."

"I wish I wasn't."

"That why you threw all that stuff out?"

"Yep." Tears welled in her eyes and she glanced away, wiping them.

"Flammable, that stuff."

She held one hand in the other, squeezing her thumb. "Thank you."

"You've already said that."

A weak smile pushed into her moist cheeks.

"W—" I began.

Something crashed from inside her house. It sounded like deckchairs collapsing all at once.

"Not again!" Pippa yelled and ran indoors.

I followed, unable to work out whether I'd seen fear or anger in her face.

We entered the kitchen first. The aroma of fresh coffee overwhelmed me. Plates and cutlery were stacked high in a sink filled with filthy water, and a scatter of cornflakes covered the counter. Into the hallway next. The layout was similar to my own and where my back room had become a library, she'd converted hers into a studio. Or at least it seemed her intention; the carpet was half rolled across the room to reveal the floorboards.

Pippa flicked the light switch but nothing happened. Desperation made her try again. And again. On, off. On, off. Click. Click. Click…

"Stop it," I told her.

The final click echoed and fell into the silence.

Evidently this was where the noise had come from.

A shrinking evening light cast a blue haze into the room. Five canvasses of varying sizes were strewn across the bare floorboards in the jagged clutches of splintered easels. Paint of all colours had soaked into the pile and peppered the floorboards. Bottles and brushes were all over the place. The black was still spreading, flowing between floorboards.

Pippa's hands twisted together. "I've so many deadlines approaching."

I didn't know what to say.

"And then all this crap happens." She squeezed tight her eyelids. "I can't handle this."

She had skill, yet the content was questionable. One painting depicted a landscape; hills and fields and a brooding sky. In the foreground an oak tree loomed over the bodies of men, their tunics clawed open around red and ragged wounds. The way some of those men held themselves suggested not all were dead. Blood soaked the grass. From a gnarled branch above dangled a woman dressed in rags, her neck broken and hooked in a noose. Such was the detail you could hear the men groan, the rope creak, and almost see the woman's body swing.

Another was of a village market square. A crowd gathered around a pyre, its flames licking the night. At its heart, thrashed an elderly woman tied to a wooden post. In the shadows at the rear of the crowd, several men writhed on the uneven paving, their faces a bloody mess. Again, such was Pippa's skill I heard the crackling flames, the woman's screams.

The other paintings depicted similar scenes of women dying; drowned, stabbed, beheaded. The latter was particularly gruesome.

I had no doubt as to who or what these women were: witches. After all that happened to me at the beginning of the year, was I again dealing with witches?

"Please don't judge me." Pippa's voice drifted over my shoulder.

I pushed fingers through my hair. It was getting long and I realised I hadn't had it cut for over a year.

"I know what you're thinking," she continued, "but I don't usually paint this kind of shit."

"You have no idea what I'm thinking."

She picked red paint from her cuff.

"Let's put it this way," I added, " I have books that delve into the history of witchcraft. I'm talking about a real history you won't find anywhere in your local library. Or online."

She crouched and pulled a canvas towards her. It was the one of a woman's limp body being dragged up a riverbank by whom I suspected to be the Witchfinder General himself—a man who in the 17th century unceremoniously tortured women suspected of witchcraft. He was beneath the shadowy arc of a bridge. The darkness that clutched the stonework churned as though sentient, its coiled tendrils extending towards the cheering men above.

Together, Pippa and I propped the canvasses against the wall and set aside the splintered easels. Her work really was good. There was something about the way she used subtle brush strokes around the figures that gave the impression of motion. There must be a technical term for it but I wasn't an art critic. She had talent, that much was obvious.

Then I found a sixth canvas, smaller than the others. My hands froze.

"What is it?" Her voice was tiny.

I stared at the painting. Of all of them, this one was unfinished—or at least appeared to be. It was a landscape focused around a wall of looming rock, moss-covered and ancient. In their shadowy embrace, dark clumps of what appeared to be fungus covered the leaf-strewn ground. But on the rock, the symbol—the *sigil*, as I'd recently learned—was barely noticeable yet it was there like some prehistoric cave painting. Faded red, a symbol of two triangles facing one another, one hollow, the other solid, and separated by a crude X.

"Leo?"

I touched my sleeve—an unconscious habit now. I should've known this would never end.

I relaxed my jaw. "These are good."

"What is it?" She demanded, her voice now even smaller.

"I…"

"You recognise it." Her chin quivered. "That symbol."

"Yes."

"What does it mean?"

"Pippa, I—"

Behind us, the floorboards creaked.

Timber groaned and split and heaved as though something pushed from beneath. Nails pinged around us. Pippa shrieked and ducked, and something stung my cheek. From between splitting planks, a cluster of shadows bubbled. Like liquid it oozed upwards and stretched as though testing the air. Faint strands coiled and whipped, spraying flecks of darkness like black tentacles flicking ink.

"What's happening?" Pippa shouted.

From my boot, I pulled out the Witchblade.

She stumbled backwards, wide eyed. She stared at the spreading darkness—those sentient shadows I was all-too-familiar with—and then back to the curved blade in my hand. "Leo?"

I stood between her and the shadows, pointing the blade towards the expanding darkness. Already the tip spat white energy. That ozone smell—something I'd almost forgotten—teased my senses, somehow comforting. This reassurance of its power was short-lived however, as the oppression of the shadows constricted not only the light but peace of mind, sanity, anything *positive*. It made me want to turn the blade on myself, to push its length through my jacket, to feel my intestines slice open... The warmth, the freedom...

I shook my head. "No!"

Pippa shuddered. By the look on her face she was having equally disturbing thoughts. She glared at me.

The shadows thickened and a thin tendril shot towards us, towards me. It snatched the Witchblade from my hand. I grabbed air as the shadow snaked back into the growing nest of darkness.

"That was not supposed to happen," I said. There'd been a time when the shadows were afraid of the damn thing.

Pippa had pushed herself against a far wall. "None of this is supposed to happen."

As though holding their breath, the shadows sucked inward and released the weapon. With a glint of fading daylight, the blade thumped an angled floorboard. It spun, then slid and came to rest on one of the straighter, untouched boards.

I started forward, reaching out.

"Don't!" Pippa screamed.

The Witchblade twitched and jumped and landed again with a clunk. As though an invisible hand grabbed it, the blade stabbed the timber...then scraped along the grain. Wood curled in its wake, nearing the spilled black paint.

My lungs tightened. All the books I'd read since the chaos at Periwick House, the sentient darkness of the Shadow Fabric, the reanimated dead, the deaths of those I'd known...all I'd learned during and after that time, was useless. These shadows were different. Sentient as before, but this was something else. And when the blade—my Witchblade—dipped into the paint and began to write, I knew this was entirely something else.

H...

"What the—?" I shouted.

H...E...

Pippa pushed herself against me, tugging my jacket.

HELP.

What the hell was going on?

ME.

"Leo?" Pippa whispered.

The blade clanked to the floor, spun once, and was still.

HELP ME.

The heaviness in the room somehow weakened, my brain clearing. Whatever supernatural Being was behind this had apparently spent its energy. The darkness had fully retreated, to bubble like a pool beneath the split floorboards. It seethed, spitting shadows like puffs of smoke.

I stepped forward and pulled Pippa with me—she still had my jacket in her hands.

"Um, sorry." She let go and straightened, seeming taller. She was still about a foot shorter than me.

Spreading my stance, I grabbed the Witchblade. Nothing happened.

She eyed the weapon.

"Let's get out of here." I told her. I didn't know what else to say, what else to do. This was her home certainly, but what could we do? And who the hell had written that message?

Once again the floorboards creaked and heaved, though not as fierce as before. Rusted nails screeched. The darkness oozed from beneath and streaked across the wood, stretched over the skirting and up the wall. It spread like damp blemishes, only thick and black.

I nudged Pippa towards the doorway. "Go!"

The door slammed just before we reached it.

Pippa actually laughed. "Of course."

More darkness blossomed. We backed up. The window was our only exit. I glanced around for something heavy enough to smash it. I went to grab an easel, and…

In a surge of shadow and brick and mortar, a portion of wall burst outwards into the garden. Twilight and cold air rushed in. Brick dust swirled. Dry, bitter.

I looked back at the door. The darkness spread across the wall and over the door panel, the knob vanishing in a twist of shadow. Whether this was a supernatural entity or even the Shadow Fabric, it seemed we had only one exit. I left the easel where it was.

"Go!" I shoved her towards the heaped masonry. "Now!"

She staggered and I gripped her shoulder, steadying her. My neck tingled, feeling the encroaching darkness. Rubble shifted beneath our feet and we made it into the garden. The Witchblade was still in my hand yet there was no energy coming from it. Cold and useless.

I had no idea where to go.

Further ahead, separating our gardens, the ragstone wall exploded. Dust and darkness bloomed, the grass heaved. Deep-rooted shadows churned in the crumbled remains. I'd seen this before, back when I'd witnessed the Shadow Fabric burst from the ground. Yet this was different, *everything* that was happening was different.

At some point I'd grabbed Pippa's hand. She was cold. For a moment I thought of heading for my house but that was absurd; there'd be no safety so close.

From the edges of uprooted ground, like some kind of black fungus, dark streaks broke across the grass, curling and bursting and mixing with the earth. Sweaty, glistening heads bulged and split, oozing black goo and bleeding into the shadows.

This was most definitely different than anything else I'd experienced.

Pippa's hand wrenched from my grip and I staggered.

She was no longer there.

I scanned the collected shadows, natural or otherwise. More of that fungus smothered the grass and weeds, choking foliage.

Her cry echoed from somewhere ahead. I stepped sideways, forward and back. Where the hell—

Beyond the crumbled wall, along the row of trees that marked the surrounding fields, a cluster of shadow thickened. Beneath over-hanging branches, Pippa's face, pale and wide eyed, stared back at me.

Her muffled cry of "Leo!" echoed as though even further away.

I leapt over the sprouting fungus. How had she travelled so far? I sprinted. Almost there, and…her body stretched with the darkness, her form rotating, churning like curdled milk. She vanished. Only to appear again further away, past the trees and in the fields. More fungus spread, and again she cried out.

I charged towards her, my arms pumping close to my body, my feet slamming hard on the uneven ground. The Witchblade spat weak pulses of energy, somehow depleted. Having been touched by the shadows, perhaps its power had been drained. I had no time to think on it.

Again in a blur of black and white her image phased into an almost ghost-like streak. Then vanished. Still I ran. How many more times will she vanish and reappear? Finally to be lost altogether? Tall grass whipped my legs. Up ahead, the sweaty heads of fungus glistened in the fading light as if to guide my way.

Pippa's silhouette ricocheted from tree to tree, merging with the shadows. Shimmering images of her leapt from shadow to shadow, across fields, appearing and disappearing. Again and again... Her screams were muted; a constant echo.

Still, I ran.

Up a gradual rise, her image flashed yet again. It clung to the natural shadows between trees. Faint at first, then her terrified face sharpened, bright in contrast to the seething darkness that trapped her.

"Help me!"

Her words reminded me of the message written in her studio. Was that Pippa who now screamed it or was it whoever had used the Witchblade to write in the paint?

She vanished.

My breath short, I made it to the tree line. More fungus ate into the foliage to mark the way. I kept the trees to my left and charged past. Into another field. Up ahead, a jagged outline cut the deep blue of twilight sky. Once a barn or some kind of outhouse, crumbled walls hid in a sea of nettles and tangled brambles. A corrugated roof, rusted and buckled, lay beneath heaped bricks and rotten timber. The fungus, the thickened shadows, ended.

There was Pippa. But—

No, it couldn't be her.

Wisps of shadow drifted over the brickwork, blending with a dozen images of her sitting on the ruined walls.

Closer, and I saw it wasn't Pippa but several different women dressed in rags or long skirts, filthy and sodden. A storm of shadow obscured their heads, hiding their faces. One had a noose around her neck while another sat cradling her arm. Another held a bundle of rags close to her bosom, perhaps a child. One of the women, whose hair dripped a liquid darkness, kicked at a black mess at her feet.

My pace slowed. I had no doubt these women were witches. Whether practitioners of black or white witchcraft, they were here. *Ghosts* of witches, and Pippa had painted their deaths.

I jogged to a halt.

As if to acknowledge me, their limbs jerked. Excited almost. Their heads swayed with the darkness that hid their faces. Wisps of shadow skittered around them, teasing. In turn, the darkness fell from their heads. Faceless. Framed by unkempt hair, their smooth and mottled flesh stretched blank where faces should be. Stretched like a canvas. Dark veins bulged ready to burst from the skin. One had her hair tied back in a red scarf, though most left it straggly and knotted. Others kept it long. But their faces. Holy shit, their faces. Or lack of.

I tightened my grip on the Witchblade and approached.

Fungus crawled up the brickwork, teasing the mortar. The black vines brushed one of the women's dangling bare feet.

As I neared the ruin, I saw Pippa. Finally.

Across an expanse of swaying nettles, Pippa slumped against crumbled brickwork. Of all the women here, she was the only one whose image was sharp, clear. She hunched in shadows that appeared to boil from the ground, her arms outstretched and bound by loops of darkness. It was like she was crucified.

I rushed forward and tripped. My knees thumped the ground.

Around me, a deepening darkness twisted and uprooted clumps of earth. Vines as thick as my forearm snaked upwards, daring me to approach further. The trunks split and black spores puffed, clouding the air.

I held my breath and scrambled up. There was no way I wanted to inhale that crap. I backed off. Shadows thickened, blackening the grass and spreading further to the left and right. More vines twisted with the earth, their lengths splitting open with tiny mouths dribbling fungus and spores. Barbs pushed from beneath grey flesh, curved and wicked.

A wall of shadow swept up, blocking my advance.

I thrust with the Witchblade. The blade sliced through the darkness and when I yanked it out, the jagged tear sucked closed again. There was no Witchblade fire, no power or strength to be gained when brandishing it; I may as well have been holding a dinner knife.

I took another step back as those vines slithered towards me. Those barbs looked nasty. Spore clouds drifted.

"Why the hell did you lead me here?" I yelled beneath my hand as I clamped it around my nose and mouth.

A torrent of shadow roared above the ruined walls, blending with the onset of night, obscuring a moon desperate to break through the clouds. Amid the roiling darkness, images flickered like TV screens. Each showed another place, another time.

"What is this?" I demanded.

...A swinging noose from an oak tree...

"Tell me!"

...Deep water and flailing limbs...

Pippa's scream echoed, muted in the darkness. "Leo!"

...Blood pouring from wounds along a slender arm pricked with needles and sliced with daggers...

Memories. Each mirrored Pippa's paintings to reveal the suffering and individual deaths of these women. Perhaps they were innocent of witchcraft or were even white witches, never using their craft for the dark arts.

As one, these phantoms raised an arm. Clumps of shadow and filth dripped from sleeves. They pointed at Pippa.

Still I couldn't advance, couldn't help her. She struggled in the embrace of a thickening darkness, stitched into the shadows. She writhed, jerking her head back and forth. "Leo!"

Beneath her the ground bulged.

I lunged forward and smaller vines whipped up. A billowing cloud of spores filled the air. And again, I backed off.

The ground shook and through the tangle of nettles near Pippa's kicking feet, a barbed trunk as thick as a telegraph pole burst upwards in an eruption of earth. The vine slumped against the wall, smashing through brick. Hundreds of barbs scraped the brickwork, rasping as they reached for her.

The scene brightened as moonlight finally peeked through the clouds. Its ambience weak yet managing to break through the darkness and roiling shadows.

It highlighted everything.

"Shit!" I shouted.

From the immense trunk, a barb had extended, longer than the others...closer and closer towards Pippa...and it pierced her wrist. Blood trickled.

Her scream filled my head.

Again, I charged forward and again the barrier forced me back. Pathetic sparks dripped from the Witchblade—still the damn thing was useless. Something was draining its energy.

One of the phantoms, her face glistening in the silver light of the moon, pointed to her wrist. The others stroked theirs, too. A few even nodded. Their freaky, faceless heads bobbed up and down in a stuttering blur. Even more grotesque now they were lit up by the moon.

"I can see that!" I shouted. I knew that barb had pierced Pippa's wrist. What did they want me to do?

A phantom shook her head.

"No?" This was insane. But fuck, I should be used to this.

The same phantom slapped her wrist, so hard I almost heard it. Slap-slap-slap-slapslap... No, it wasn't her wrist, but her forearm.

"What?" Then I knew. I knew without a doubt what these dead witches referred to. I pulled back my sleeve to reveal a scar where once I was branded in the shape of the same sigil Pippa had painted.

I shouted at them, my voice a roar: "This?" I held up my arm. The skin itched and burned like fresh sunburn. What precisely were these phantoms telling me?

Pippa still thrashed in the embrace of the shadows and coiled vines. Another barb had pressed into her other wrist, and blood trickled down her hands to drip from clawed fingers. Her clothes were filthy, smeared black with mud and fungus.

At her feet, in front of the slithering vines, the shadows bloomed and opened up.

An image flashed.

I blinked.

The unfolding darkness lightened and wavered like a poor-quality video. Then sharpened, in and out of focus to show something familiar: Pippa's scattered paintings and spilled paints. I watched as I had earlier, the Witchblade—the Witchblade from the *past*—write HELP ME. Only this time a ghostly hand visibly gripped its hilt, the knuckles gnarled and arthritic, liver-spotted and wrinkled. The image panned back to reveal the frail and hunched form of another witch. Her stained clothes, no more than rags bound by frayed rope, were caked in mud, thick like clay. Across thin shoulders draped a dark patchwork shawl, leathery and rumpled. She released the blade and as before, it dropped to the floorboards. The crone stepped back and turned and looked directly at me.

I jerked and coughed, and I hoped to hell I hadn't inhaled any of those spores—although their clouds had calmed now I'd stepped further back.

Tiny eyes, darker than the surrounding shadows, glared through a mass of spider-web hair. Her nose was a fleshy lump above the thin slit of a mouth that curled into a twist of scar tissue. Once upon a time she'd been burned. Badly. I thought of Pippa's market square painting; the one where the witch writhed in roaring flames. Was this her whose form now shimmered as she reached the edge of the shadows? Was this a portal?

The darkness shuddered. She stepped through into the present.

Shadows sucked at her and there she stood. Nettles smouldered and shrivelled, crumbled dead at her feet. Even the earth blackened. Smoke and shadow curled into the air. She lifted her head and eyed the Witchblade in my hand. Her lips twitched, the webbed scar silvering beneath the moonlight. Twitch-twitch, twitch. Was that a smile?

The Witchblade—the Witchblade of the *present*—jerked and a warmth spread up my arm. Traceries of white fire spat from the blade. Still its power was limited. I gripped tighter. The same white energy skittered across the crone's shawl, weaving with the stitches between each patchwork section. It seemed to writhe, charged with new power.

Then it all made sense.

"You crafty bitch," I shouted.

Already having sufficient power to snatch the Witchblade from me in Pippa's studio—somehow twisting time, too—this crone had harnessed its energy. Leading me here, she'd then channelled the energy so to transport herself from the death, the *hell*, she came. The way her form shifted and shivered, edges fuzzy one moment and sharp the next, suggested this was only part of her resurrection.

Another piece of this puzzle was Pippa.

She was still framed by the great hulks of vine, barbs secured into veins. Waves of shadow braced her shoulders and bound her arms. Her head lolled, her eyelids droopy as though she was drunk. Soft moans drifted towards me.

Seeing her like that made me feel so damn helpless.

The crone, of all the other witches, was undoubtedly the most powerful; evidently the only one present with such power to cheat death, even though she'd been burnt at the stake. Her shawl moved as though the wind was fiercer than it was. A patchwork of fabrics…brown, dark, stained. And it moved, contradicting the crone's own movements as she approached Pippa. It was alive, pulsing. *Breathing.* The darker patches reminded me of the Shadow Fabric, the way it shifted like spilled diesel. The crumpled sections, some kind of animal hide, had been stitched with it.

Then I knew precisely who this crone was. How she'd accomplished all this I hadn't a clue, but I had no doubt of her identity.

Belle Mayher. A woman who was said to have lived beyond the age of 250, noted to have stitched the largest sections of the Shadow Fabric. The very Fabric that would later be unleashed across London in 1666, before the Great Fire. Her powers were unparalleled and included the unique ability to absorb others' powers and abilities. She had been—still was?—in league with an entity known as Clay, Demon Stitcher of Shadow and Skin. Human skin, not animal hide (to demons we *are* animals). Selling your soul was not a myth; she'd done precisely that. And she wore proof to the fact.

I could only assume she was at this very moment absorbing Pippa's artistic skills. To what gains, I had no idea. I knew for certain, however, she was even now absorbing the Witchblade energy; that's why its power was weak.

A cold wind bit through my clothes and I shivered.

The other phantoms had retreated. Some huddled against each other. The one with the baby shook uncontrollably. Fungus grew from the rags she cradled. The closest phantom whose feet dripped dark water, frantically waved her forearm and it was as if I heard her yell for my attention...even though she had no mouth. She made sawing motions across her forearm.

Was she telling me to cut myself?

I raised the Witchblade.

She stopped sawing and her faceless head jerked in affirmation. Dark splashes flicked upwards.

I didn't want to cut myself, that was absurd. My scar, shaped like an hourglass, had become part of me and this dead witch wanted me to cut it. Not a day had passed when I didn't drag my fingertips over the lumpy twists of skin, thinking, remembering... I guessed I'd always be connected to the darkness that we humans are so ignorant towards. It's always been there, and always will be.

The crone, Mayher, had grasped Pippa's head in one hand and a barbed vine in the other. Blood gushed from her serrated palm. Her lips moved, chanting some witchcraft bullshit. Her shawl surged and writhed about her shoulders, energised.

Moonlight reflected from the blade I held before me. I could only guess that cutting myself would somehow reenergise the Witchblade, to steal the power back from Mayher. I pressed it, warm, vibrating, against the scar and quickly sliced along the outer edge of the sigil.

A thin line blossomed red, oozing. Entirely painless.

From across the ruins, the crone's dark gaze struck me. My hand froze. Her lips peeled back over broken teeth and she hissed louder than the wind.

Now I bled, having done what I'd been instructed—advised by a dead witch, for God's sake—what the hell was I supposed to do now?

I lifted my arm and shook it.

Blood spattered and disappeared onto the blackened ground.

The fungus quivered, the grey heads lightening, breaking apart. I waved my arm around, the blood pouring out—worryingly a little more than I'd hoped. But it worked. The fungus shrivelled and crumbled. Swiftly, quicker than I would've expected, the clumps dissolved. The air no longer tasted as tainted as before, and I stepped forward over the dead ground. Blood dripped down my forearm, my fingers now slick.

Pippa's body no longer moved. I hoped I wasn't too late.

The shadows had even retreated.

"Ha!" I yelled into the swirling masses as they drifted away.

I ran towards Pippa and Mayher. Fungus puffed into harmless dust beneath my pounding boots. The nettles and brambles and grass broke away with the crumbling fungus, leaving dead ground, mud and dirt.

The crone's scar twisted ugly and she glared at me, eyes a wicked Stygian darkness. Her shawl seethed around her shoulders, the patches squirming and glistening. She shrieked.

It drilled into my brain and I staggered. Colourful zigzags pressed in on my vision, threatening to yank me into the shrivelled tangles of blackened nettles and grass. Witchblade fire spat and charged, red and orange and yellow flares lit my way. Finally, I had control; I had the blade's power back in hand. My muscles flexed and I straightened.

Still Mayher shrieked, hunched and buckled over as the faint energy drifted across her shoulders and down to clawed hands. White charges spat from her fingertips. She'd lost control of that stolen power.

I leapt and booted her in the chest.

My foot passed through her…but slammed into the shawl. It flew from her and slapped the brickwork. It fell, twitching in the still-dissolving fungus.

Mayher staggered backwards as though I'd succeeded in kicking her. Her ephemeral form shifted and slid from focus, merging and churning with the broiling darkness. Her shriek was now dampened, subdued by the retreating shadows. Through weak, grey eyes she looked down at her shawl.

Part-flesh, part-shadow, the foul garment writhed on the ground. Patchwork sections had come undone and the flesh seethed, rippled. Blood oozed from torn stitches, and frayed ends of shadow squirmed as though desperate to be threaded once more.

Defying the shadows that embraced her, Mayher rushed for me. The darkness shredded.

She yelled and swiped at me.

I crouched and swung my arm up to block, ready to thrust with the Witchblade. Her gnarled fingers passed through me.

Hair rose on the back of my neck.

Behind her, the darkness thickened. Dense tendrils whipped around her neck and torso to snatch her backwards, her heels digging into the ground yet leaving no mark. Her eyes flared. The shadows were determined to take her back into death. She struggled, throwing glances at her shawl that bled into the cracked earth.

Pippa still hadn't moved. Still the barbs were rooted in her veins. The shadows that bound her wrists drifted away yet the vine held her upright. They hadn't dissolved with the rest of the fungus. Being as trunk-like as they were, I guessed they'd be the last to respond to whatever power my blood contained. This was new to me; all this was a different kind of weird.

I reached Pippa and stabbed those massive trunks. Witchblade fire, white and brilliant, rushed towards the barbs that punctured her skin. Black filth bubbled and oozed from the wounds and the barbs slid free. Harmless to us, the fire roared and enveloped the trunks. The thick flesh blistered, stinking and smouldering. They thumped the ground and deflated, shrivelling into twisted coils of muck.

Pippa flopped into my arms. I propped her against the wall. Her eyelids flickered and she murmured something.

Mayhar's scream pulled me upright.

The phantoms were all now animated, their faceless heads turned to the crone as she kicked at the shadows. The other witches were clearly fearful of Mayher which led me to believe she'd somehow collected them here to reinforce her resurrection. I could only assume she'd absorbed their abilities and crafts even in death.

Mayher had somehow reached her shawl, now clutching its patchwork remains together. Gore dripped from it in clumps, black threads dangling.

I jumped up. Witchblade fire erupted from the blade and I rushed towards her as again she attempted to strike me. A darkness flickered behind her eyes as though energised once again by the shawl. White energy flared from the blade and shot into her face. Again, this witch burned. 350 years beyond her death, after a failed resurrection, fire ate into her skin once again; Witchblade fire she failed to control.

Her scream tore through the countryside.

I swiped the blade downwards into the shawl. It sliced through the fabric. Shadows bubbled and flesh bled. The crone retreated. She flailed, desperate to hold on to the garment. Again the shadows snatched at her.

Pippa was pushing herself to unsteady feet.

"Go!" I shouted at her.

She scrubbed the blood and filth from her arms and succeeded only in smearing it. Her hair obscured her face.

The shadows were diminishing, and the fungus shrank to become little more than grey goo. So too were the remaining vines, crumbling to dust.

The phantoms whipped the shadows into clouds and as one, they swarmed Mayher. A blur of ghostly rags and skinny limbs flew down on the crone. Glimmers of faces, eyes and noses and mouths appeared—some of them were attractive, or had been in their day. Pretty faces, whether innocent of witchcraft, whether practitioners of white or black arts, they had been released. No longer were they the forgotten faces of the 17th-century witch trials.

Mayher struggled beneath the onslaught of phantoms and deeper shadows that surged around them all. A wall shook and collapsed in a rush of brick dust and lingering shadow. I had no idea what the ground would do given that the fungus was shrivelling and the vines crumbled.

"Run!" That word had become too familiar. Ever since the evil behind the shadows had returned, ever since the hell that had occurred at Periwick House, I'd shouted that a lot.

So we ran. With a final glance over my shoulder I saw Mayher and the phantoms vanish in a vortex of shadow.

Moonlight swamped the area, cleaner, fresher. A dust cloud caught on the wind.

We sprinted across the fields. When we were safe, I looked at Pippa.

Just like the phantoms, she had no face.

DUE SOUTH

The barbed wire tore across the back of Robert's hand and he staggered away from the fence. He watched blood rise and pool along the wound. Somewhere nearby a crow cawed as though laughing.

Mud sucked at his boots.

It was his own fault. He should've walked further, keeping to the fence and eventually a stile to cross. At least he still headed due north. He pocketed the compass and map, and pressed a thumb to the wound. Mabley Holt was still an afternoon's hike away. It had been a long time since he'd met up with Carl. In fact, Robert guessed the last time they'd seen one another had been his fortieth birthday. Carl had booked a table at a restaurant called Periwick House, a retreat apparently known for its excellent food.

Blood smeared the back of his hand pink but the wound no longer bled. He grunted. Perhaps it hadn't been as deep as he first thought. He squinted at it; now more like a scratch.

Careful to avoid more barbed wire, Robert squeezed through the splintered fence and into the next field. As he followed the jagged chasm of tractor tyres, he puzzled over the wound. It itched. He rubbed it, glaring as though willing it to cease the irritation. Should he be worried about tetanus?

On he pressed, treading through woodland where autumn had already stripped the trees naked. As he walked, he swigged water and occasionally made certain the compass needle still pointed north. Such was the light, each time he checked his course he brought the compass closer to his face.

Eventually hunger tugged his stomach. A Mars Bar cured that.

Heavy mud clung to his boots and caked a stile as he pulled himself up. Straddling it, he stuffed the chocolate wrapper in a pocket. Ahead, nothing but fields and woodland. Beautiful.

He dropped to the other side and scratched his hand—something had irritated the other one now. Perhaps he'd caught it on brambles or nettles and not noticed. Some kind of allergy maybe. He rubbed his hands, his knuckles, and knotted his fingers together. More scratches—were they scars?—what the hell was this?

A glance at his watch revealed 2 p.m. But that couldn't be right; it had been that time when last he looked. So his watch had stopped—bloody brilliant. He took out his phone: 5 p.m.

His stomach lurched. How had the time passed so quickly?

Given the surrounding hills and rocky countryside, he wasn't surprised to see there was no phone signal.

Off he trekked again, now at a faster pace.

Soon a darkening sky pressed in. He had planned to reach the restaurant before nightfall but that was not going happen. There were still five, maybe even six, miles to go. This was crazy. Perhaps over the next hill he'd get reception and then phone Carl. Thinking of Carl annoyed him further—it had been his choice of venue, the retreat in Mabley Holt. Granted, Robert took this as an opportunity to get into hiking again after several years away from it, but even still…if only Carl hadn't chosen a village in the middle of nowhere then none of this would be happening.

Robert squeezed the back of his neck. He really should've driven like most people.

Soon he walked parallel with the trees and then with a stream that curled into the woodland. The darker sky and those looming trees pressed in.

His hands, even itchier now, fumbled open the map. It was as though he'd rammed them into nettles, elbow-deep among stingers. While scrutinising the route ahead, he guzzled water. And spat it out. Bitter, disgusting. It dribbled over his lips. He hurled the bottle down and water gurgled. With a yell that shocked him, he booted the bottle. Tangled branches swallowed it in a murky spray.

"What the hell—"

He yanked out his phone: still no signal.

Gripping the phone in his fist, it felt warm, getting warmer by the second. A sticky mess oozed between his fingers. The battery had leaked? Seriously? He rammed the phone into a pocket.

"You have got to be kidding!" His voice bounced off the trees and came back deadened. He wiped sticky fingers on his jacket. At least the compass still worked. For now. Thinking that, he knew he'd be screwed if the needle seized.

Shadows thickened, pulling darkness closer, and he slowed his pace. He dragged his hand, burning, from forehead to chin. Hungry, thirsty. His hands shook. A series of scars crisscrossed his knuckles. Even as he watched they stitched across his fingers as though a thousand invisible razorblades danced across his flesh, yet immediately healed. That now-familiar burning sensation rushed over him, the heat surging into his head. It had to be some kind of allergy. He saw what they actually were: not just lines, but arrows.

"What—" The word tumbled over dry lips.

Arrows scratched, *etched* into his skin. Pointing... They pointed in the opposite direction: south. And when he moved his arms more scars formed in his flesh...again, pointing down towards the tree line, and the stream.

His scalp itched. He clawed at his hair and grunted. In jerking, frantic movements he slung his bag to the ground and yanked off his jacket, then his jumper, unconcerned as the clothes caught on brambles. He barely felt the cold as he tugged his T-shirt over his head.

Scars webbed his skin, up his arms and across his chest, his stomach. Bright white and stark in the failing light. Dozens— hundreds—of arrows glistened. Burning agony.

His scream echoed once. Again, a dead sound.

He stepped towards the field, in the direction of the hill. Surely there would be signal up there and then could call emergency services. Sod Carl and the restaurant, he needed medical attention. Now.

And he remembered the battery had leaked. His heart plummeted.

Each time he stepped towards the stile another arrow cut into his forearm, others on his biceps. As they appeared, he hissed, cold air rushing between clenched teeth.

"Shit! Help me! Someone! Please!"

Each arrow pointed towards the trees, and when he staggered and flailed his arms, the arrows moved to point back at them once again. And again.

The sound of water echoed. Beckoned.

He dropped to his knees, then collapsed into an awkward sitting position. He waved his arms before tear-streaked eyes. Agony seethed across his flesh as more arrows tore into his forearms. Still no blood, but the pain... He kicked at a lone fence post, and shuffled through the grass and mud.

His breath sharp in his lungs, he pushed up onto unsteady feet. His boots felt miles away as he dragged them through clinging mud. Darkness pressed in. His head throbbed.

And his flesh burned with agony.

With eyes half-closed he followed the sound of water.

The stream widened into a shallow pool to trickle between mossy bulks of rock. Beyond this was the pond, dark, uninviting. Little of the remaining daylight penetrated the patchwork of leaves overhead.

He scrubbed and scratched at his hands, wringing them together. They now bled. Slick. Pieces of his flesh caught beneath his fingernails in dark curls.

"God," he pleaded, "help me."

He leapt towards the rocks, smacked into one, and crouched at the water's edge, arms outstretched. Cold, soothing water splashed. Perhaps he laughed. From behind, trees groaned. Something snapped—cracked and echoed. A branch crashed to the ground in an eruption of leaves.

Robert's leg shot sideways and he sloshed into the water, instantly soaked. Freezing.

The ground heaved and he rolled over, gasping. His hands slapped the water, but the relief...oh, the relief was wonderful. Sitting in the water with knees up near his elbows, he waved his hands beneath the surface. Cold, welcoming. He rubbed his torso and arms, and felt the lumps and ridges of a thousand scars.

His vision blurred. Then sharpened.

On the other side of the pond, the rocks and tree trunks shimmered. The darkness shifted and seemed to toy with his perception. Shadows closed in as though night suddenly fell. They squeezed his view across the mud and the water. The shadows churned. In teasing wisps they swept up, down, left, right, as though trying to grasp something. No, not grasp something, *become* something.

An outline of a figure, eight, nine, ten feet tall. The silhouette glinted like a reflection in broken glass. With muscular arms and legs, its slightly-hunched form held firm a wide head that sported three jagged horns. Shadows curled from them, and traceries of flame spat and crackled.

The stink of smoke, heavy vegetation, and something else, cloying, something dead, scratched his throat and stung his nostrils. He coughed.

The thing towered over the bank, red eyes glowing through the swirling shadows.

Silence and…

Fence posts splintered. Barbed wire whipped the air, whistling, and wrapped around the creature's limbs. The barbs tore into its flesh, black blood oozing. The shadows retreated and it stepped forward. Glowing scars criss-crossed its chest and abdomen, sparking as though each leaked an inner fire. It raised an arm, a fist that unfurled, palm up. Offering…

Scars covered its palm.

Robert's body ached, the heat still rushing over him. In his head he screamed, in his head he *ran*…but the mud sucked at him, the water froze him.

Carmine eyes burned from the creature's bulbous head.

Trees creaked, more wire whipped the air, more fence posts snapped as the shadows behind this thing gaped wider.

A heavy darkness, smothering shadows, rushed outwards like a tsunami and washed over Robert. Heat without agony. And for that, he was thankful. His flesh entwined with the darkness, and shadowy fibres sliced into his arms and body and face. Curls of his skin interlinked with the shadows as they raged around the creature.

Warmth bathed him, and the darkness soothed him.

Other forms shimmered and shifted in the darkness, and he knew they were like him; those lost and forgotten over centuries, summoned as fuel to an ultimate goal. He sank into their phantom arms, the broiling darkness enveloping him.

The creature's form snatched more branches and rock and rusted wire. As the shadows stitched to embrace Robert, he sensed elation. The creature, this Being, would finally tread the Earth after a millennia of imprisonment.

RED, WHITE AND BLACK

Judy only knew his first name: Charlie. And he was dead.

He wore the same white clothes as her. Itchy and loose. White sneakers, too. Or *trainers*, as they said here in England. Only his, toes down over the bed, were spattered with blood. So much red in contrast to the glaring walls. Red, white...and black. A tar-like substance clung to the bed linen and spotted his clothes, merging with the blood. Clumps of that dark filth streaked the wall as though it had grown from the plaster.

The medication, the drugs, whatever they'd given her, still clogged her brain, and even a cry for help seemed beyond her.

She stepped back and her ass smacked the door frame. A lump filled her throat. She swallowed and breathed. She'd become accustomed to the institute's fresh paint smell but now the coppery stink of blood overpowered it—and also something like wet foliage or soggy vegetables.

The sheets were twisted around his body, his face pressed into the pillow. That black stuff streaked his neck and cheek. Whatever it was, it looked like it had suffocated him. His hands were dead claws. His arms, hairy and bloodied. Welts and blood-bruises curled around his forearm.

Just like her own.

She brushed her knuckles down her arm, over those peculiar welts and grazes. Still sore, and still she couldn't recall how she'd gotten them. Similar to Charlie's, yet showed no sign of any black infection. Was this going to happen to her?

Earlier at dinner, he'd invited her to his room saying he had something for her to read—which could mean any number of things. However, she saw a newspaper heaped beside the bed and had no doubt that was it. The front page pictured a man wearing sunglasses, his face turned to the headline: DEATH OF A HERO. Above that it said, *John Lennon Shot Dead in New York*.

She snatched it up and stared at the portrait photo of her favourite Beatle. He wore a blazer, a shirt, and a loose necktie, and he looked smooth in those sunglasses. Shot dead? Her hands curled into fists and the paper crumpled. She tore her gaze from the newspaper, back to Charlie. The dark filth also caked his hair.

At least she couldn't see his face.

Her cheeks were warming, her breath quickening. Again, her thoughts dragged.

The last time she'd seen him alive, he had a spoon of pudding in his mouth and waved at her across the canteen. Her head ached and she'd needed to lay down. Everyone had responded differently, and she guessed that was the nature of a clinical trial. The doctors told them they'd be monitored over the next several weeks. She looked at the black muck, the way it oozed from his wounds. Whatever this was, it was one hell of a side effect. Perhaps other candidates had also died. She had to find someone, tell someone. She twisted the newspaper in her hands and the welts on her forearm appeared to wriggle—her vision pulsing like it had during dinner.

She had to get a grip on herself.

Charlie was dead. Lennon, too. This was a sick world she lived in. Lennon, murdered in NYC. Her home, her city. The ceiling seemed to press down, lowering until it almost touched her scalp, the main house above pressing her into the earth. The thought of being in Britain—in the Garden of England, no less—felt truly absurd at that moment.

The newspaper slipped from her hands and fell with a slap. She blinked, focused, and her sneakers squeaked as she lurched into the corridor.

She called: "Help! Anyone? Help!"

Her voice shot along the strip lights and bounced back. Then silence.

The floor tiles sucked her feet and she staggered onward. She passed another room and a peek revealed a kaleidoscope of red, white, and black. She wasn't surprised. Her ill-fitting clothes flapped as her pace quickened. More rooms, each no different from Charlie's. Her head throbbed with every footfall. Just how long until this caught up with her?

She shouted, "Hello?"

Again, silence.

"Hell—"

From somewhere a burst of static answered. The sound crackled and faded.

An empty corridor led to another stretch of open doors, every one revealing more death. And that black infection. The trial had clearly gone wrong.

Around a corner, along another corridor, Judy reached an area she'd often thought of as a reception. Usually there'd be a nurse or an orderly busying around. She approached the glass-fronted office—a smear of pink and grey misted the cracked glass.

Inside, a computer terminal with bulky casing took up most of the desk. A telephone, receiver missing, sat dwarfed by a stack of manila files. The coiled wire draped across a lady's wrist. One blue fingernail pointed in accusation at a black smudge on the desk.

An earthy stink filled Judy's nostrils. She held her breath and took another step forward.

Slumped in a swivel chair was the nurse, Mary. Or May. Judy almost felt guilty in forgetting and refused to get close enough to read her name tag. Those familiar shades of gore covered the woman's uniform. Her neck stretched, head back, hair dangling to the tiles. Her white hat rested in a red pool. That black matter splayed across the tiles.

Perhaps this had nothing to do with the trials and was instead some kind of outbreak, some fatal disease.

A sound—rustling?—echoed from further down the corridor. Another survivor? Thank God.

Her vision warped and she stumbled, backing out of the office.

A rustling, shuffling sound, again and...

"Have you seen Kat?" A man's voice erupted from behind her and she spun and almost collapsed into his arms.

Parker.

His eyes, piercing, blue. His hair, ruffled. Sweat beaded his forehead. "Judy. Where is Kat?"

Often this doctor—she'd assumed he was one of the important doctors behind these trials—would bring his daughter in. A cute child, about four or five years old with flaming hair and inquisitive eyes. Judy focused on the room beyond him. Colouring books scattered the floor and crayons were crushed into the tiles like rainbow splinters.

"Have you seen her?" He grabbed Judy's shoulders. Along his forearm, running parallel with his veins were familiar black marks. No red welts though. He released her and stepped back. He shouted, "Kat!"

Shaking her head sent silver spots darting across her vision. She straightened her back. "What's happened here?"

"We have to find Kat."

"Yes. I'll help. Why is everyone—"

"Dead?"

She nodded. More silver spots.

"We must find Kat." He charged towards the double doors. With palms flat, he shoved them wide and disappeared into the next room.

Judy followed. It was kind of like a classroom, where she and perhaps a dozen others sat when first introduced to the trial ahead. She'd sat at the back next to Charlie—dead!—whom at the time she'd not known. They were all there for the same reason: money. Judy recognised an eagerness in everyone's eyes, and wondered if she looked the same. Clinical trials offered a lot of money these days. Apparently it had something to do with the patients already here at the institute but although Parker gave them a tour, they weren't allowed to see any patients. Prohibited access, he'd said and added that they were expanding departments.

Across the room, Parker yanked open a door to a stationery cupboard. Swinging wide, the handle thumped the wall. He hardly resembled the confident doctor who'd once stood before them, smiling and concluding that most of the underground sprawl here was an immense building project.

Judy felt useless, her mind reeling. This was all like a bad trip, feeling just as she had last year. Unlike some of her friends who spiralled into the madness of drug abuse, she'd been lucky to escape her teens. This had been the beginning of a new life for her. At least, that was the intention.

Parker barged past her and out of the room. "Help me."

She pressed her palms to her temples and followed. "Sorry."

In the corridor, his mouth turned down at the corners, he shouted, "Kat!"

Music crackled from somewhere like a radio had been switched on. It came in faint waves. Judy couldn't make out the tune.

Parker frowned and headed for an archway, into another corridor. "Kat?"

His pounding footfalls echoed and Judy staggered after him. Her stomach somersaulted but at least her vision was sharpening. Into the corridor, those strip lights a harsh glare, she squinted. Parker had vanished. Three doors lined a wall. The paint smell filled her nostrils and somehow cleansed her mind. Only a fraction.

A door creaked. She rushed for it and pushed it open. Her vision blurred. The wood was cold—even that seemed to clear her head a little more.

Crouched between filing cabinets, hugging his red-haired daughter, was Parker. He said her name over and over. Her arms wrapped around his neck and in a tiny fist a crayon poked between her fingers. A black one.

In a muffled voice, she said, "Daddy, where is everybody?"

He didn't reply, only squeezed her.

High in the corner of the room more of the black filth peppered the walls and ceiling, resembling damp spores. The house above was old so she guessed the foundations would be just as old. Surely where they were expanding the underground part of the institute, damp spores wouldn't set in so soon. In truth, she had no idea.

Parker stood, lifting Kat into his arms. His smile said everything.

Kat's eyes were wide and round. She still clutched the crayon. "Hello," she said to Judy.

"Hi." Judy held the door open for them.

"Right," Parker said, his voice stronger than before. "Let's get out."

Her brain still felt sluggish. "What's going on?"

"I have no idea."

"But—"

He led them back to the office, and made sure to face Kat away from the dead nurse. This time, Judy was close enough to read the name tag: Mary. The black stuff coated most of it, and appeared to have melted the plastic.

Snatching the telephone, Parker prodded the buttons. After a moment's pause, he said, "Dead."

Judy again glanced at Mary.

Parker scratched his forearm. "We must assume it's taken everyone else."

"Why not us?"

He pulled Kat into his arms. His eyes seemed to shrink and he looked down. "Come on."

They ran through a set of double doors, passing through several empty rooms. Beneath an archway, they entered a room unfamiliar to Judy. She assumed this was one of the prohibited areas.

Hypodermic needles lay scattered on the floor. Again, black marks streaked the tiles. Further back, the strip lights bathed a row of gurneys, the linen seemed to glow. One was occupied by a man, naked from the waist up and secured by wide leather straps. That black matter caked half his torso. His eyes bulged and blood covered his shaven head and smeared his cheek. His lip flopped between clenched teeth from where he'd bitten it off. Black filth glistened, protruding through torn flesh and broken bone like the stuff had risen from his throat and busted through his jaw. Even now, it dribbled from between bone splinters and bubbled onto the mattress. A tooth bounced and tittered across the tiles leaving bloody splashes.

What the hell was all this? Why had the three of them been spared? Parker had those marks on his arms, and her own red welts didn't look good. This was some kind of nasty infection, certainly. It was simply a matter of time. She hoped Kat would somehow be immune.

The doors on the other side of the room swung closed with a double slap. Alone. Judy's heart twisted and she threw herself at them. She entered a wide room and an overpowering smell of paint washed over her. Although familiar throughout the institute, in here it poured down her throat.

Kat stood beside her father, watching him pick up a crowbar.

Overturned paint tins littered the floor, their contents puddled from wall to wall. White, glistening, and fresh. A stepladder lay on its side, and footprints headed off beneath an archway and round a corner.

Parker lifted Kat with his free arm as Judy reached his side. Creating footprints of their own, they followed the other set to the corner.

And stopped.

Judy's breath snatched and she coughed.

"Don't look," Parker said to his daughter.

The body of a decorator huddled against the wall; his legs trapped by a mound of grey-black filth, his neck a ragged mess. Bloody handprints smeared the wall. Above, more filth—*fungus*—drooped from a hole. Finding a larger amount of that black matter, Judy now saw that it was indeed a type of fungus. Exposed wires coiled through its sweaty skin. They sparked.

That music again; a distant sound, crackling.

The strip lights buzzed, then surged and went out.

Kat screamed.

The yellow glow of emergency lights flooded the corridor.

The fungal growth above seethed, the shadows deepened, and the black mass rushed downward. Tendrils burst from its surface, flexing dozens of skinny fingers. One extended and with a wet slap, coiled around the decorator's leg to yank the body towards the ever-widening darkness. It was as though the shadows had opened up like a gaping mouth. The light dimmed further as the fungus clawed across the ceiling, the walls, the floor.

Parker held Kat away from the expanding darkness. A slithering tentacle whipped out, lashing for him. He swung the crowbar and the thing recoiled like a snake.

He shoved Kat into Judy's arms. "Take her!"

Judy hugged the child to her breast. More darkness splayed across the tiles, blending with the paint, the blood. Reaching out. This fungus had a life of its own. Impossible.

Again Parker swung the crowbar and his leg shot sideways. He crashed to the floor and scrambled to his knees, slid, and smacked the wall. The tendrils drew back, ready to strike a second time.

"Come on!" Judy shouted and with one arm, yanked him upright.

Deep furrows creased his forehead. "Run!"

Judy fled down the corridor and in seconds reached an intersection.

From close behind, Parker yelled, "Go left!"

More fungus coated the walls and encased the occasional strip light. Sprinting beneath it, heading along that stretch, the darker the corridors became. Judy waited for the darkness to thrash at her. How was this happening? What they'd witnessed back there had been impossible.

After what seemed like a hundred corridors, they reached the elevators. The strip lights were all dead and the emergency lights pushed through deep shadows.

"What—" Parker began to say, and he staggered to a halt. One hand pressed against a wall, his chest heaving.

Kat's tears soaked into Judy's shirt. Her lungs burned and when she stepped closer to the elevators her stomach lurched. The fungus had stitched the doors together. Black fibres entwined like stubborn roots.

"Bloody hell!" Parker's knuckles whitened as he twisted the crowbar.

"The stairs?" she demanded. Kat was starting to feel heavy.

"There aren't any." His eyes narrowed.

"What?"

"We're far below ground. Only the lifts."

Lifts. She loved the British.

"There's another lift...on the other side." He pushed past her. "But I don't fancy the walk."

He raised the crowbar.

For a moment he paused, and again Judy heard the faint crackle of music from somewhere. As before, she couldn't quite make out the tune.

"Parker..." She breathed out, not realising she'd held her breath. It was as though she waited for that black stuff to come alive and grab him. She stepped further back.

He stabbed the crowbar between the elevator doors, leaned against it, and heaved. They didn't budge, nor made any difference to that fungal growth. He heaved again.

And the doors burst open.

A dark expanse of simply *nothing* lay beyond. A kind of liquid darkness shimmered like a diesel spill defying gravity. Parker tumbled headfirst into the yawning void. This time the blackness didn't look like fungus, it looked like the shadows themselves had opened up.

The doors slammed closed. Black threads crept inward and with a sound like dry leaves, stitched the doors together.

"Parker!" Judy backed up, turning Kat's head away and hugged her tighter. The weight of the girl brought the darkness closer. No stairs.

Judy turned and ran, heading back towards the intersection. She had to find the other elevator, wherever the hell it was. The fungus already crawled over the tiles, along the walls. Sure, there were scuffs from the gurneys, but the new flooring, the bright white walls, the brilliant glow of those strip lights, all highlighted the creeping spores.

She shoulder-barged a set of double doors and lurched into another room. Her heartbeat seemed to echo in the emptiness. From an archway at the far end, music drifted towards her. Recognition. It was a Beatles tune: Hey Jude... John Lennon was dead. Shot dead—she still couldn't believe it. So many thoughts crashed through her brain. Her arms ached and her legs felt like jello. She slowed her pace and stopped before the archway. On the other side, another corridor; bright, white, and no darkness. There didn't appear to be any spore patches, either.

She placed Kat down.

Hey Jude…

The girl looked up at her and then around the room. Wide eyed, red face, puffy. Her cheeks glistened. "Where's daddy?"

Judy swallowed, her mouth and lips dry. "He's… He'll be with us soon." She hated herself for saying that.

The music seemed not too far away. Jude, Judy… Her father used to call her that, before alcohol made him call her other things, before alcohol forced his hand against her mother. She recalled how once she'd had to clean up blood from the kitchen floor. That slap and swish creating pink arcs, the radio playing in the background as she wiped away Mother's agony. Slap, swish.

Judy lifted Kat and headed off, praying she'd find the elevator soon. As she rounded a corner…

Slap, swish.

Diluted blood smeared in an arc. And that sound: slap, swish. Beside a bucket overspilling with pink froth was the janitor, mop in hand. His blue uniform flapped around him. Blood splashed his shoes.

The strip light overhead flickered, and in a burst of static the music faded.

Slap, swish.

Judy's pace slowed. Finally someone else was here, someone else to help.

Kat's tiny arms looped Judy's neck, and in a muffled voice she said, "I want to walk."

"No," Judy whispered. They were only a few paces away from the janitor. She hoped he wasn't contagious and moved closer to the wall. "Help us," she said to him.

Still he kept his head down. His voice croaked as he said, "I must clean this up."

"Help us!"

"It's that damned harvest."

"What?"

The blood left little room for them to pass.

"Such a mess," he said and raised his head. White teeth shone through a bushy beard, his hair just as unkempt. "Stevenson and his damned harvest."

She had no time for this. "Which way—"

"Stevenson. The boss. Not the boss-boss, but the boss down here." Sweat dotted his brow.

"What are you talking about?" she snapped.

He pushed his hand against the wall. Spores bloomed from the surface, approaching his fingers. His flesh darkened and a greyness crept under his sleeve, up his neck and into his face. His mouth went slack and his eyes moistened, then blackened. They shone like black marbles. No white, just solid black orbs bulging in hollow sockets. Between pale lips, his teeth flashed again.

She pressed against the opposite wall, praying that the spores wouldn't reach for her.

He removed his hand from the wall and gripped the mop. Slap, swish.

She squeezed past.

"Such a mess." He continued to mop the floor, but only succeeded in slopping the blood around. His efforts hastened. Pink water splashed the walls, consumed by the spores.

Slap, swish... Swish, swish.

The sound of the man's frantic cleaning faded behind her and the music crackled into play again.

Hey Jude.

By now, Judy's throat pulsed with its own heartbeat. Her arms were killing her—putting Kat down seemed like a good idea but she couldn't. She had to find the other elevator.

The music increased in volume, the notes sharper, the vocals more defined.

Mind reeling, she reluctantly placed Kat down. The girl's feet tiptoed and then she stood on her own. The square tiles warped and shrank. They seemed miles away and vertigo tugged at Judy's legs, her stomach. Kat peered up from far away, her eyes wide, just as Judy closed her own into a welcome darkness, albeit brief, private. Paul McCartney's vocals floated towards her in waves. She straightened, eyes remaining closed. This was crazy. And someone was playing with her, playing that Beatles tune over and over.

"What's your name?" Kat's voice leaked through the darkness, nudging aside Paul's chorus.

Inhaling the smell of paint, she opened her eyes. Kat's hair, waves of orange and red, burned through the threatening darkness.

"I'm called Kat," she said.

"I know." Judy's voice sounded weird. "I'm Judy."

The little girl nodded. "Where are we going?"

"Getting out of here." She stroked Kat's cheek—clammy— and then lifted her up. The girl somehow weighed more than she had earlier.

Still that tune crackled from invisible speakers.

Kat fidgeted in Judy's arms as she jogged through more rooms. All empty save for the odd gurney or two, all showed signs of that black stuff coating the wall. The music swept along with them, sometimes soft, sometimes loud. Always crackling, as though played from scratched vinyl. Perhaps it was from a record player. High in the corners, she saw several brackets and wire coiling from holes. No speakers.

The smell of damp, of foliage, eventually overtook the paint smell, and the strip lights seemed to be either off or not working. Only the emergency lights guided them. It appeared this was where they were still building the place. Some walls were just plasterboard panels and the ground was simply bare concrete. A wheelbarrow contained three paint tins and a bucket of paintbrushes. Perhaps given time, they'd build that staircase. She guessed—she *hoped*—the elevator would be somewhere near.

Then the lights went out. Deep, dark, suffocating.

Not even any emergency lights.

Kat screamed. It echoed, shrill. Her fingers dug into Judy's neck.

"It's okay," she told the girl, stroking her hair. She didn't know if she reassured Kat or herself.

The music had stopped, and so had they.

Something creaked—a door?—from beside them. A vertical strip of light speared the darkness; a pathetic illumination.

Kat made a mewling sound like an animal.

The door swung wide and smacked the wall. The echo died as the music resumed, this time from within the room and no longer crackling. A miasma of damp, decay, and that heavy stink of vegetation forced itself down into her lungs.

Beyond the doorway, a vortex of yellows and browns churned and filled the room from floor to ceiling, wall to wall. Sweat prickled Judy's forehead as she struggled to comprehend what she faced. Kat clamped to her neck. Even though Judy thought of how the elevator doors had jerked open and swallowed Parker, she couldn't move. She had to, but couldn't. Whatever this was it curdled like mud and oil, milk and gravy. It hurt to look at, yet was mesmerising.

Still the music washed over her.

Judy squinted, knowing she must run. Amid the roiling chaos, the colours merged and twisted like teasing shadows, like phantoms in a sickly mist. Contours formed, sharpened; outlines of something…of furniture? Yes, a table and chairs, walls and picture frames. The haze thinned out, the browns becoming yellows and spiralling into cleaner colours, pleasant, soothing, *normal*. Sharp, three-dimensional and familiar.

Way too familiar.

Hey Jude…

She licked her lips. This was a dining room, *her* dining room—or at least, her parents' dining room.

A remaining coil of shadow swooped down and around the turntable of the stereo system. Darkness spinning, coiling with the rotating vinyl. Faint wisps joined it and vanished into the stylus.

Her heart felt like a brick. What was this? And the music filled her up, stormed her ears.

The doorframe seemed to buckle, swept up into the surrounding shadows, torn apart silently. She stood in the centre of the dining room. The tune rose in volume, rumbling from the twin speakers either side of the record player. From the direction of the kitchen she heard Mother preparing dinner.

Judy realised she was holding her breath and mouthed, *No*.

Kat released her leg. "Where are we?"

Judy blinked. When had she set Kat down? She didn't recall letting her go. She stepped forward. "Kat…"

The girl stood beside the oak table, its scuffed surface still marked by the red paint Judy had spilled—oh, how father had struck her hard.

She threw glances around the room.

Kat walked further forward and looked around. She passed straight through a chair as though it wasn't there. Of course it wasn't there, none of this was real. Everything was a cruel phantom, a tease from Judy's past, a taunt of a childhood she so desperately wanted to leave in New York. This all had to be due to the clinical trial. Some bad trip, a hallucination triggered perhaps by the chemicals she'd abused in her teens and now the ones the doctors had given her.

She lifted her arm and looked at the welts and blood-bruises. What happened to her?

The little girl continued to walk and passed through the table. Her hair seemed to glow in contrast to the illusion. Through the table, passing the red stain that was now fading—wisps of shadow rose like smoke. Kat turned and lowered herself to sit on something Judy couldn't see. Whatever it was, it made her bounce. Perhaps it was a cushion under the table—but this was all an illusion. The now-shimmering mirage of the table almost obscured the girl.

Judy moved, her eyes darting to the left and right, over to the fading archway. The clatter of cutlery, of dishes, reverberated from beyond. Her mother was there.

Her tongue stuck to the roof of her mouth.

Hey Jude…

Kat looked up as a shadow emerged from the kitchen. Someone approached. It wasn't Judy's mother, couldn't be. Her mother was dead, killed by her father. Could it be her father? No, impossible, his suicide had closely followed.

Judy felt as small as Kat. The drugs they'd fed her were really playing with her, dragging up unwanted memories.

The bulk of shadow filled the archway and finally someone emerged. She couldn't see the face. A white smock, stained dark, somehow pushed aside the wispy shadows, the image, the illusion. Lights flickered around the figure—candles, there were candles. No longer lampshades, and not even strip lights. Just candles.

Her phantom past, the music, all shrank and dropped back to where it belonged: the past. None of this should be here. The room faded, and in its place the rocky expanse of a cavern stretched out, its gloom lit only by the candles. Moisture dampened the air, ammonia stung her nostrils. Where was she? As the final wisps of shadow lifted, the false room completely vanished. This appeared to be the end of the labyrinth of rooms and corridors beneath the institute. Rock and masonry heaped the floor, and a number of concrete pillars reached into the darkness overhead. A stretch of unpainted wall lined one end of this great chamber. The blank-faced plaster looked out of place, foreign next to the curved, dark hulks of rock. The candles flickered, their haloes offering little comfort.

"Hello." The man's voice pierced the gloom. Deep, commanding. She recognised it. It belonged to Stevenson, the boss, the man in charge of the trials. This was the second time she'd met Stevenson. The first was when she'd sat in the room with the other candidates, when she'd signed the consent forms thinking only of the money.

Judy raked her fingers through her hair. Her head ached.

"Did the darkness make you see something?" he asked.

Judy glared at him. She didn't know what to say. None of this made sense. Earlier the janitor had said something about Stevenson's harvest. What had he meant?

"Hello, Kat." He smiled and slid his hands into his pockets.

Kat said, "Hi." Her back was twisted as she peered behind her and stared up at the man. She sat on a stained mattress. Leather straps, like serpents, coiled next to her. The buckles glinted with a dull wink from the candles lining an outcrop of rock. The archway behind Stevenson—no longer the archway to the phantom kitchen—framed him. It made his presence even larger, made him loom over Kat. Over them both.

The man approached. His moustache twitched.

"You're Judy," he said.

She nodded. "What's going on? What have you done to us? Everyone else is dead. Are my hallucinations anything to do with you? The trial?"

"What did you see?"

"We have to get out of here!"

Something clanked.

Kat had reached behind her and now dragged something over the mattress. "What's this?" She pulled an hourglass into view. Scuffed wood, scratched bulbs; the thing looked ancient. What appeared to be a wrist harness swung from it. Its buckles clanked again.

Stevenson's grin pushed his mouth wide, thick lips glistening. "That, young lady, is the hourglass." He put emphasis on the word *hour*.

Kat clutched it and looked into the lower bulb. She shook it. "It's old. What's it for?"

"Put it down," Judy yelled. Whatever it was, it was unnatural. And Stevenson had a hand in all this. "Don't touch it!"

Kat shuddered. Her bottom lip quivered.

"No need to be like that." Stevenson stepped around the mattress and stood beside a computer terminal that squatted on the floor. Wires and cables poked from it. The blank screen reflected the hourglass and Kat's tiny hands. "It's a method of extracting darkness."

"What?" Judy's voice sounded tiny even to herself.

The little girl's chin trembled, tears welling.

"The clinical trial is only half of it. This…" He waved his hand over Kat's head. "…Is what really matters."

Judy crouched beside the mattress. She took the girl's hand and whispered, "I'm sorry."

Kat said nothing, staring into her lap. The hourglass rested against her thigh.

"There's a darkness within us," Stevenson said. "Within us all."

"We have to go." Judy grabbed Kat's arm. "Come on."

Stevenson's voice drifted over her shoulder. "That magnificent device allows us to tap it."

Pain. Sharp at the base of her skull. An explosion of colour…

Then nothing.

Tangled images threaded together and Judy struggled to make sense of them: shadowy tentacles snatching Kat's father into the elevator; the janitor mopping blood; black spores spreading across the walls…and the turntable, spinning round and round and round. Hey Jude. The black void swallowing her.

Judy's consciousness sharpened, and now the sound of creaking leather, of clanking buckles, drifted through the dark. Her eyelids cracked open. Wide.

The air snatched in her throat.

She lay on her side, the cold ground biting through her clothes. Her ankles were bound to her wrists, her back hunched. Rope dug into her already-enflamed flesh. She recognised the rock walls and the archway a short distance from her. And the mattress.

Kat was on it. The girl's eyes were closed, her breathing rhythmic as though she slept—unconscious but alive. Her legs and arms were spread, wrists and ankles fastened by leather straps. One tiny hand curled around the lower bulb of the hourglass, secured by the attached harness. The computer hummed and a series of commands ran down the green screen. Bunched wires coiled from the main unit and connected to electrode pads that stuck to the girl's temples.

Judy's heart lurched. "Leave her alone!"

Stevenson stepped into view. "You're just in time."

"What are you doing to her?" she demanded and tried to kick out, only to succeed in sliding sideways. Her back hit the rock wall. "She's just a girl!"

"Yes, that's why I'm seeing what her darkness will be. Your coming here is a stroke of luck, wouldn't you say?"

"Let us go!"

"The hourglass will connect with her darkness," he said. "It's a 17th-century device once used to extract the evil from supposed witches."

"What?" Judy struggled to sit up. Failed.

"A remarkable apparatus," he added.

She glanced at her wrists, the rope binding them, and those welts, the pinches. Her stomach knotted, and she knew that she'd once been attached to this hourglass. "You're…you're behind the infection."

"It could be a type of infection, certainly." He shrugged and glanced at Kat. "But it's more than that."

Judy wriggled. Her back ached and her head thumped. It felt sticky from where Stevenson had evidently knocked her out. "This is madness."

"Darkness is the root of our madness."

A wave of nausea rushed in on her. She gulped, refusing to spew. Her breath came in gasps. She had to save Kat.

"That's right, calm down."

From an angle, Judy saw chalk markings on the rock face beside her. Words? Symbols? She didn't recognise any. One, however, could've been a crude diagram of the hourglass itself. Silvery spots peppered her vision. Those markings blurred for a moment; they looked like real voodoo crap, some kind of occult bullshit that belonged in those absurd Hammer horror films these Brits seemed to love. Gritting her teeth, her ears ringing, she focused on Kat, and on the hourglass. The white sand in the lower bulb looked innocent enough. Perhaps extracting the darkness would somehow cleanse her, or would it infect her? But she was only a child. And what did this darkness have to do with madness? Again, Judy struggled against her bonds.

"Why are you doing this?" she shouted and kicked.

"We need to wait a while longer, then we can begin." He watched the computer monitor. "Not long."

More commands scrolled down the screen.

Judy thought of what the Janitor had said. "Something to do with your harvest?"

Stevenson's eyes narrowed. "You shouldn't know about that."

"Is it?"

"Most likely, yes." He again glanced at the computer. "Okay, we have time."

He crouched beside her. From a pocket he pulled out a Swiss Army knife, then cut her ankle bindings.

"Come with me." He grabbed her still-bound wrists and yanked her up.

She grunted, pain burning the back of her head. With a final look at Kat—so peaceful—Judy swayed.

Stevenson tugged her beneath the archway. Still gripping her arm, he threw open a door with his other hand. "I'm proud of this."

She squinted as a dozen or more spotlights burned into the gloom. The stink of vegetation, of rot, of mould, reached down Judy's throat.

"That idiot Parker never even knew," Stevenson whispered.

Judy's stomach twisted. "Oh my God."

Beneath metal framework, four gurneys lined a wall. Naked bodies occupied them. Male or female, she had no idea. Every mattress was stained brown and dotted with dark spores. Clamping apparatus held open the chest cavities where fungus growths bulged. Like gigantic black slugs, throbbing—with a heartbeat?—they seethed and converged overhead amongst the frame. The skin glistened and reflected the spotlights. Most of the ceiling had vanished in an expanse of sweating grey-black flesh, pulled taut like a grotesque canopy. Spores peppered the floor and the spotlight bases, the walls and the remainder of the ceiling.

Stevenson smiled.

Something—someone—groaned.

"Dear God, no," whispered Judy.

One of the bodies twitched and the head moved. A man. His eyes wandered as though drunk and his agony hissed through clenched teeth. Fungal tentacles swung from his chin.

Beneath his gurney, a darkness clustered in wispy shadows. A coiling pseudopod heaved and slits along its length puffed more spores, more shadows, to cloud the air. It hurt to look at; the way it kind of played with reality. Even as she watched, another tendril of shadow reached up to clutch the ceiling. It shifted aside the tiles. One fell and smacked the floor, cracking in two.

More pseudopods whipped the air, again the slits opening like mouths and belching clouds of shadow.

"Beautiful, isn't it?" Stevenson left her in the doorway and strolled into the centre of the room. He held his hands wide. "I have discovered the darkness inside us all."

Tendrils slithered towards him and stroked his shoes. This fungus had a life of its own, so did it know this man was its creator? Did he control the fungus, the shadows? Chasing his own desire to find the darkness at mankind's core—the very heart of madness—he'd clearly gone mad himself. Perhaps he'd inhaled the spores or even the shadows that now puffed from more slits along the tentacles. Did he once attach himself to the hourglass?

Judy gaped as the sentient clusters of darkness caressed his legs.

Those dark clouds were similar to the shadows that earlier had coiled from the phantom record player. She'd been attached to that hourglass at some point during her stay here, of that she had no doubt. That's why the shadows had revealed her past, it was her own darkness tangled with unwanted memories; a madness waiting for her.

She had to stop this. She had to rescue Kat before the computer loaded and the hourglass began whatever it was going to do to her.

Judy held her breath, hunched, and darted forward. Her shoulder smashed into Stevenson's stomach and he stumbled backwards. Driven by momentum, she almost went with him as he crashed into a gurney. The overhead frames screeched across the floor, and the fleshy sacks ruptured. Great plumes of shadow and spores fluttered. And embraced him.

He didn't have time to scream.

Only his feet and one arm stuck from the quivering mass as it ballooned. The other gurneys shifted and the clamping mechanisms snapped closed. Shreds of black flesh flapped about and muffled the crunch of breaking ribs. Brackets and rods sprung sideways, clattering off the tiles. Some hit the fungus sacks with a thump. The main mass, once supported by the frame, had drooped. Metal groaned, shrieked, then snapped. The bulbous thing collapsed and slapped the ground.

Slime splashed Judy's face as she rolled away.

A seething yellow goo spread across the tiles. Pseudopods whipped and jerked, lashed and clawed at the tiles.

She scrambled to her feet.

More clamps pinged and clattered across the room. One of the bodies fell with a wet thump. A splay of black matter leaked from the gaping stomach. The dark clouds, the *shadows*, reached out—almost as if in comfort.

Stevenson's legs vanished.

Judy, cursing her bound wrists, staggered. She slipped, almost went down again, and lurched for the door.

Making it round the corner and beneath the archway, she dropped to her knees beside Kat. A glance at the computer and it appeared as though the column of data was slowing. She tugged the wires and the electrodes popped from the child's head. The screen went blank.

From behind her something else clattered, the light from the doorway shrinking. Without looking, she knew the pulsating mass of whatever-the-hell-it-was filled the doorway. Or perhaps it was the shadows. She fumbled the straps that fastened Kat's ankles, releasing them. Then those at her wrists. No time to remove the hourglass harness. The device thumped Judy's leg as she scooped up the girl and hoisted her over a shoulder—awkward with bound wrists. The rope pinched.

She backed out from the chamber, into the dark corridor, and jogged beneath the welcoming glow of emergency lights that looped from bare plasterboard panels. The elevator had to be here, or maybe another exit somewhere.

The area widened into an unfinished mess. The plasterboard gave way to rock either side. Further ahead where girders lined the ceiling and pushed into rock, a chain-link fence stretched out and separated them from a construction area.

Kat flopped in her arms and the hourglass smacked her thigh. Judy began to limp, heading for what she assumed was a chained gate in the fence. Perhaps they'd be able to squeeze through. Beyond this, deep in shadow—natural, she hoped—were what looked like pallets piled with bricks. Yes. There were bags of cement, too. There was even a forklift truck. There had to be an exit that way.

Her legs were killing her and her arms screamed from awkwardly holding Kat.

She knew the darkness spread behind—her skin itched like a million ants crawled over her. The closer she got to the fence, the more she saw a faint light far on the other side of the construction area. Yes, she'd made it. No elevator, but sunlight?

Two horizontal stretches of light cut through the gloom. From a pair of huge metal doors.

"What's happening?" Kat's muffled voice sounded sleepy. "It hurts."

"Nearly there." Judy coughed. Thank God Kat was okay.

"Hurts!" the girl whined. Blood covered her hand and dripped from the harness, the hourglass swinging.

And Judy tripped.

Her kneecaps smacked the ground, an elbow too. The girl tumbled from her grasp and sprawled, crying. Her eyes glinted in the brightening light, face screwed up.

A familiar crushing dizziness washed over Judy. She pressed the ground with her bound wrists and tried to get up.

"Run!" she shouted.

Kat stared past Judy's head. Her eyes widened and she screamed.

Judy pushed herself up, head swimming, and scrambled to her feet. She grabbed the girl, yanked her upright.

"Run!"

Staggering, the two of them crashed into the fence. Not quite a gate. It rattled. Judy's fingers curled around the chain. Cold. No way through. Her heart punched her throat. Her knees throbbed. She tugged the padlock. Locked. Closer to the ground there was a gap, big enough for Kat to squeeze through.

"There!" she yelled. "Under there!"

Kat obeyed and pushed her body beneath the fence. The hourglass went with her.

A glance over Judy's shoulder revealed the darkness clawing the rock walls. She looked back at Kat, who in turn stared up at her through the mesh. Her hair clumped across a grimy forehead. Red circles marked her temples from where Stevenson had attached the electrode pads.

"Run!" Judy poked her finger through the links in the fence, pointing at the sunlight. "That way."

With a quivering jaw, Kat turned and ran. The hourglass scraped along the ground like a medieval toy. Her footsteps echoed.

There was nothing at hand to break the padlock. Still the darkness spread across the rocks, flowing and tracing the contours, reaching for her. A combination of liquid shadow and black seething fungus crawling at her, plunging her into a deeper gloom.

She shook the fence and dropped to the ground. She pressed herself against the gap, shuffling sideways, willing herself to shrink. She clawed the ground.

Two fingernails broke. Pain exploded up her hand.

Around her, the light dimmed. The darkness closed in.

Far away, Kat shoved open the huge door. A metallic shriek rang out. The setting sun flared around the little girl's silhouette and for a moment she swam in blinding orange, the hourglass trailing behind.

Judy stopped trying to push through the gap. Kat was safe, that was all that mattered.

As sunlight swallowed Kat, the darkness swallowed Judy.

INTENSIVE SCARE

My fingers curled around the glass tumbler, and my knuckles whitened. For one absurd moment, I chastised myself for not painting my nails that evening. Candles reflected in the glass, diluted with a darkness filling to the brim. It churned like liquid, bubbled, and swept up and into my eyes. Blinding. The stink of rot—like that time I'd forgotten about the salmon in the refrigerator—clawed up my nose, down into my lungs, tainting me to the core. Gravity snatched me, and my sight returned in patchwork flame and shadow.

Gritty floorboards thumped and pain exploded through my ass, my shoulder blades, my head. Darkness claimed me.

Nothingness.

When eventually I came to, my friends' faces hovered in the dark, pale as ghosts. Their shadows flickered behind them, crawling across peeled wallpaper and damp bruises, brushing cobwebs.

"Catherine?" Becca's piercings glinted in the candlelight. Her latest, the nose stud, looked raw.

Liz, whose bleached hair obscured her wide eyes, said nothing.

I scrambled upright, away from Becca's furrowed brow, away from Liz's penetrating gaze. Away from their clutches. What the hell happened? I pushed myself to a crouch and then stood, legs shaking. Gravity threatened to claim me once again but somehow I straightened, even managed a smile. I backed away from the Ouija board. This had all happened because I'd been stupid enough to accompany them into the derelict mansion. That building of cold stone and urban legend, too tempting a place for such a game to be ignored. These girls were my best friends, and just as foolish.

"I'm fine." I coughed and my heart raged into a thunderclap. Once, twice, tearing through me, rattling my ribs.

The glass tumbler smashed on the floorboards. A hundred candle flames glinted.

And I died.

I don't know how much time passed.

Now, I stand beside a hospital bed watching my shell suck at a life-support machine. My dark hair, like splayed fingers, clutches the pillow. My eyelids cower in hollow sockets, my body thin beneath a gown as pastel as my flesh.

Where are my parents? I guess Becca and Liz are home with their families. I wonder how my story was told.

The surrounding walls fade into crushing darkness, warping shadows like torn fabric. My feet lift from the floor—I wear the same clothes as I had on the night we'd entered that building. Shadows embrace me. I am with the Darkness…and his arms are fire. Hot, pure. With him, I fly, and we return to the mansion. As one.

There, three girls, one called Catherine, sit cross-legged around a Ouija board.

The Darkness sees an escape.

The girl called Catherine snatches the glass tumbler…

MEETING MUM

"Rachel?"

Derek's new girlfriend sat on a patio chair facing the darkness of the empty swimming pool. She couldn't reply because she didn't have a mouth. Nor could she look at him because her eyes had also vanished. Her flesh glistened, taut as though pulled over a balloon. Traceries of dark veins throbbed beneath.

Her head tilted, and although faceless begged for help.

His breath snatched on the chill air and he dropped the bundle of fish and chips. It slapped the paving like something dead.

Beyond the reach of patio light, the trees and shrubs crouched in shadow. They seemed to embrace his periphery, squeezing his focus on Rachel. Her green dress hugged her body, wet with sweat, and her legs stretched out before her. One foot was tangled in some kind of fungus with twisting vines that reached from the darkness of the empty pool. A peculiar smell drifted off her, like mixed spices and cooked vegetables. Heavy. It reached down his throat and he choked. His vision blurred, his mind rushing in waves.

He blinked and regained focus.

They were due at his parents' house in an hour. Finally they'd meet Rachel. But he couldn't let them see her like this. No choice now but to cancel. Mum especially would be disappointed.

He stepped away. Beneath his boots, soggy paper split. Another step and he kicked chips and fish and strips of batter. Coughing, he went indoors and prodded the light switch. Darkness stole Rachel away. He slid a hand into a pocket and removed his mobile. His thumb twitched as if in defiance when he brought up his parents' number. Yeah, Mum was going to be pissed.

Dad answered—thank God—and Derek gave his excuses. Ill, he explained, Rachel had come down with something. Which in truth wasn't a lie.

The rest of the evening he spent alone on the sofa, staring into the TV. The images flashed across the screen. Motion, colours, sound; nothing made sense. He didn't go into the garden again and eventually fell asleep.

Come morning, forcing himself outside, Derek squinted into a reluctant sunshine. It was as though the sun refused to highlight the black fungus that bulged from the middle of the empty pool. Crawling vines with floppy sacks like deflated footballs clung to the filthy paving. Several tiles were cracked, and shards littered the patio. Rachel sat with the pool's gaping emptiness before her as she had the previous night. Dark and thorny vines still tangled with her leg. Those strange black sacks pulsed. Like they breathed. She didn't move as he came to stand beside her. The stink of rotted vegetation stung his nostrils.

He placed a hand on her shoulder—slick, warm.

"Rachel?"

Still no response.

The vines, those *creepers*, had fused with her leg and even now writhed. Where they speared her skin pus oozed, dribbled. Raw, angry. Her head hung, just a dome of veins and festering sores, and her hair had fallen out.

His hand slipped from her shoulder and swung by his side. Indentations remained from where he'd gripped her. The veins beneath rippled and the skin smoothed out. A small voice, muffled yet screaming at the back of his mind, told him this was an infection, and to get out of there, to run, run far away…and why the fuck wasn't he running? But he didn't understand that need, couldn't run, hide. He couldn't leave her. Neither could he allow Mum to see her like this. Yesterday Dad suggested should Rachel feel any better, the pair could instead come over tonight. No chance.

The vines squirmed, rasping. Black stuff oozed.

Derek called work and said he was sick. And he probably was. He spent the day watching nothing on TV and neglecting his rumbling stomach. Neglecting Rachel, too.

Late afternoon, something crashed outside.

His vision dragged across the room, colours blurring. He stood, giddy. It took several seconds for his brain to catch up. What was wrong with him? He felt hung-over. Finally his head cleared and he ran through the house, into the kitchen. His shoulder slammed the half-open patio door and he almost slipped on the wet ground—it had rained during the day. Puddles merged with creepers that were now as fat as his thigh.

Rachel…

Her dress was now a darker green, blending into puffy flesh. It was difficult to tell where she ended and the fabric began. The grey vines almost entirely covered her leg and blended with a trunk of a root that disappeared into the heaving mass in the pool. The crash, Derek could only assume, had been the side of the pool collapsing to make way for more bulging sacks. Cracked tiles and earth cradled the bulbous hulk.

An electronic warble, ringing, tore into the garden. It sounded strange, alien.

His phone.

Numb fingers fumbled and he answered.

"Derek?" Mum's voice.

"Yes."

He squeezed the can of Coke he didn't realise he still held. Empty. He let go and it landed with a thud on a vine trunk. The surface rippled.

"Are you coming over tonight?" Mum asked. "I'll make a roast. We have chicken."

Rachel's flesh, crispy, looked like roast chicken.

"…Vegetables…"

Rachel smelled of vegetables, with that cloying spicy tang.

"…Yorkshire pudding…"

Rachel's shoulders bulged similar to a lump of batter, irregular and browned.

"Mum, I—"

"Come over tonight, eight o'clock. No excuses."

"But—"

"Both of you." She clicked off and the silence swallowed him.

Approaching seven o'clock, and Derek held an axe.

His fingers curled around the wooden handle, slick with sweat. He stood over Rachel...or what remained of her. Beneath the gleaming skin, those traceries of veins wriggled like a hundred worms. Several creepers were wrapped around her arms, and fungus covered her right hand. The main trunk, the one that wound its way from the empty pool, throbbed as though it breathed.

His eyes drifted from the seething mass in the pool, along the length of trunk, and to Rachel's squirming flesh. He lifted the axe high—it swayed, heavy—and swung it downwards.

The blade sliced the trunk with a squelch.

A tar-like substance burst out and soaked his trousers. The severed ends whipped, stretching sinew and mucus. Both ends writhed like battling snakes spraying black venom.

Backing away, he almost slipped in the spreading goo.

Rachel shifted sideways. Her body slapped the ground and the chair skittered across the patio. The trunk flopped back into the crumbled mess of the pool.

Derek's heart hammered so loud he didn't hear the axe drop. He knew he should run, leave her, but he couldn't. His mind clouded. He grabbed Rachel's leg, sticky, slimy, and he gripped tight. He lifted her up. Awkward. Black stuff dribbled from her stump. One step after another, his back screaming, he hefted her alongside the house, beside the garage. A wind hissed through the conifers lining the driveway. They swayed as though drunk. The security light surged as he approached his VW. He squinted. The boot was already open, the compartment gaping like a mouth. The silver bodywork glinted. He wedged her inside, bunching up the creepers and quivering sacks as best he could. Black goo smeared his bumper. He rummaged behind her, feeling for his toolkit. Tugging it free, he popped the clasps. Cable-ties, where were they? He knew he had some… Finally, yes, here they were. He fastened two around her oozing stump.

He reached up and gripped the boot. The metal was cold and for the briefest of moments, his mind cleared. *Dear God, what was happening? He had to call an ambulance, and…* And the darkness closed in once again.

Framed by a curl of prickly vine, Rachel's faceless head peered up at him as though saying: "Your mum's gonna be pissed at this."

The sound of the slamming boot echoed.

On the doorstep, Dad eyed him up and down. "Been working in the garden?"

Derek lifted his hands and stared at them. Muddied and smeared black with fungus they seemed far away, strangely detached. "Yeah," he said. His voice sounded far away, too.

"Wasn't a bad day before it started raining." Dad wore his usual yellow jumper. The porch light shone from the dome of his head.

Derek nodded.

Dad's gaze floated over Derek's shoulder. "Where's Rachel?"

"In the car."

"Mum really wants to meet her."

Behind Dad was a framed picture of the three of them on holiday in the Mediterranean: Mum and Dad with a seven-year-old Derek. They all held hands, smiling.

"I'll go and get her," Derek said.

Back out to the car, boot open, he lifted out Rachel. The blue-black veins wriggled beneath her flesh that was only just visible through the coiled vines. Her head flopped sideways, that blank face reflecting the orange glow of a streetlamp.

With his back killing, he carried her into the house. He didn't even think to wipe his feet.

"We're out here!" Dad's voice came from the garden.

Derek staggered outside.

Mum sat on a wooden chair facing the pond. It wasn't often he'd see her in anything other than a floral dress and tonight was no exception. Her head jerked and twisted to look at him. She was faceless; her once wrinkled flesh taut and mauve, glistening. Her white hair, caked in black slime, clung to her neck. That all-too-familiar fungus coated half her torso.

Derek dropped Rachel beside his mum.

In the corner of his eye, a black mass swelled in what remained of the pond. He stepped back as a vine slithered free from his mum's legs.

Rachel's oozing stump twitched and thumped the ground. Once, twice. The cable-ties snapped from the twists of green-black flesh and flew into the garden. One hit the fence. Her stump stretched, wet and slick, towards Mum's creeper.

Those two feelers, like tentacles, were much closer. They slurped and reached for each other, squelched and finally met.

SEEING IS BELIEVING

Simon told us about seeing the darkness and none of us believed him. You know the type; the drunk bloke at the bar, the guy you have to at least acknowledge when you're up there getting drinks. Towards the end, I don't think he once took a shower. Or washed his clothes. Kev and I had always called him Sad Simon.

It began several weeks ago as he sat on his stool. He was excited about laser eye surgery. He announced it to the entire pub, which was weird because none of us knew him. Usually he remained quiet, sipping his one drink of the evening. He'd saved up enough, he told us, been wanting it for years and was finally going for it.

Apparently, and this had him in hysterics when telling us, he'd opted for enhanced night vision. That didn't mean he'd be able to see in the dark.

The next night he sat there wearing sunglasses, his head high. When he removed those glasses, I saw his bloodshot eyes. Demonic. It was the surgery. He said there was some light sensitivity but could cope, so we shouldn't worry. With eyes burning behind those shades, he explained the elation at being able to read his bedside clock. None of us cared. Kev and I continued to mock the poor bastard behind his back.

Jenny was the first he spoke to, one to one. I overheard something about a darkness that follows us. She was a good-looking girl. She had a tattoo on her wrist; a yellow circle with a smiling face inside, nothing special.

Sad I never got to ask her about it.

A few days passed and when Simon came into the pub, he was grubby like he'd been sleeping rough. Since the operation this was the first we'd seen him without sunglasses. His eyes were still as red as you'd imagine the Devil's would be.

Simon's outburst filled the evening, shouting about the darkness he saw. Everywhere, he said, all around us. The landlord ignored him, didn't even tell Simon to quieten—I'd seen our landlord shout down every potential troublemaker. I guess Simon must've spoken with him, changed him in some way so he wouldn't throw him out.

The way I think he changed Jenny, too.

That was the same night Simon touched me. The back of his hand brushed my knuckles as he pushed his empty glass across the bar. My vision briefly darkened and the overhead lights seemed to flare. And that was what changed me. Why me, I don't know.

Last night when Jenny came in, she wasn't her usual self. She didn't even acknowledge me, though her tattoo still smiled at me. It was then I realised I liked her.

The first time I saw the shadows they warped the air behind her head, a shimmering cloud of grey. She stood in the corner near the juke box watching a game of pool. The darkness flickered and inside there was something else, difficult to see.

The pub was packed and no one else saw it. I knew it was only me. My hands shook and when I set my drink down it almost spilled. Jenny's eyes were sad and it was as if her face reflected shadows. I squinted as the darkness shrank…then vanished. It was as though it gave up trying to show me something. I watched her for a while, puzzled and thinking of the exchange she'd had with Simon. What was that he'd said about a darkness that follows us? She went to the ladies room.

Kev, sitting beside me, didn't see anything. He was busy eyeing some girls as they walked to the bar. And there was Sad Simon, his eyes burning into mine. His mouth twitched at the corners. He knew. It was only me and him.

"What is it?" Kev asked me.

Pulling my gaze from the man at the bar, I focused on my friend. A darkness seethed behind his head too, only there was a faint image within those black wisps; his face dripping blood.

My breath snatched and I coughed. I tasted smoke and like a TV switching off, the image vanished. I pushed my glass away and closed my eyes.

Kev said something else but my personal darkness blocked him out. When my eyelids parted, there was Simon still staring at me. Shadows were behind him now. They showed me his face, his eyes pouring blood, his flesh peeling and curling away.

My stomach catapulted and I thought I'd be sick.

Just as it had with Kev, the vision snapped off.

There was a strange silence in my head, the urge to spew subsiding. I dragged an unsteady hand down my face.

A door slammed and the sound yanked me upright. It was Jenny staggering from the toilets. Behind her, the shadows had returned but this time it was different. It wasn't only me, others now saw them. People screamed, leaping from their seats; stools and tables upturned in a collection of thuds and crashes. Everyone charged for the exit, shoulder to shoulder, pushing others out the way. Their cries filled my head.

Billowing like curtains, the coruscating darkness bunched up and folded around Jenny. Her face twisted and she thrashed in its embrace. Her piercing scream ripped into the chaos of the fleeing crowd. The shadows collected, pulled at her, and in seconds her body vanished.

Only the shadows remained. Their surface shimmered like a diesel spill.

My head swam as blood roared in my ears.

Kev shouted something, started pulling at my clothes. He pushed me towards the door. My legs failed me and I sprawled across the table. Drinks soaked my shirt.

The shadows whirled and something white pushed outwards, reaching for me and Kev. It was an arm, and I recognised the smiling face tattoo. There was only Jenny's arm, nothing else of her, stretching from the darkness. She clutched something.

A knife. Ornate and magnificently crafted.

Still without seeing the rest of Jenny, the shadows surged. Her arm rigid, the knife pointed forward. Kev shouted, shoved me sideways, and the knife thrust into his face. Jenny's fist pumped the knife in and out. The sound of that blade stabbing, sucking and splashing into his screams overtook the cacophony of everyone's escape.

Kev collapsed in a red mess. Life rushed from him and pooled around his body. His leg twitched then was still.

I snatched my eyes away. The shadows were receding, shrinking into a tighter darkness. Jenny's hand still clutched the knife as the shadows closed around it. Only her arm remained, just above the elbow, hanging in the air.

With a crunch and red spray it dropped, thumping the floor.

My vision blurred.

The fingers still clamped the knife, the tattoo smiling at me.

I think I whispered her name.

The blade, glistening red, sparked as if something ignited. Flames spurted from the blade and caught the carpet. Spreading outwards, catching the furniture. Unnaturally swift.

Simon now stood beside me. He held two broken bottles. The overhead lighting glinted from the jagged edges.

He rammed one into each eye.

Blood splashed me and I blinked it away. My stomach was ready to lurch upwards.

He twisted the glass into his sockets. That grinding and slurping sound was all I heard. He yanked them free, threw them aside and dug fingers into those twin holes. The mess oozed down his face. It dribbled over his gaping mouth, down his neck and soaked his clothes. He tugged at flaps of skin and peeled them away.

I remember the sound as they slapped the floor.

Simon muttered something but the shouts of the remaining few to leave the pub drowned everything. That, and my heart stampeding my skull.

Finally I rushed for the exit, fire biting my heels. I lurched into the street, coughing and tasting smoke. Chest heaving, hands on knees, I spat.

When I looked up I saw the crowd around me. Their eyes tore me down. And playing in the air behind their heads were the shadows. It was only I who could see that darkness. Whether it was tomorrow, next year, or fifty years' time, I saw their death.

One was a fiery plane crash, another was peaceful but alone in a care home. There was cancer and diabetes, and all kinds of disease. There were car crashes and cycling accidents, there was a mugging and a stabbing…but not with that ornate knife Jenny had.

Death surrounded me.

I sprinted home.

That was yesterday. And that darkness is still there now, flickering behind every person I meet. My mother, my father—I know how they're going to die. No matter where I go those shadows exclusively reveal how everyone dies.

This morning I went into the bathroom and looked in the mirror. It was instinctual. Inside the shimmering folds of darkness that floated behind my head I saw myself holding that beautiful knife—the one Jenny used on Kev's face—and I am thrusting it into my abdomen. I twist it, pull it out halfway and then push it further in. Blood pumps over my knuckles. My jaw is relaxed and I do not scream. Nor are my eyes closed; they are like black marbles. It's as if they focus on something, or perhaps some*where*, else.

I fall to my knees. My shallow breath fills one last red bubble while still that knife continues to work its way inside. My eyes remain open.

The shadows embrace me.

DISTURBED

Pete gulped from the flask. Water dribbled over his chin, cold, refreshing, and trickled down his neck. Behind him leaves rustled and twigs snapped. He turned to watch Kirsty duck beneath a branch and enter the clearing. She shrugged off her rucksack and let it slump on the grass beside a row of grey mushrooms. Mud caked her boots and the hems of her jeans. She unzipped her jacket and stretched. Midday sunlight glinted from her watch as she raked fingers through her hair. A blond curl rested on her nose.

He squinted. "How about a camping trip for the honeymoon?"

"No chance, mister." Her lips twitched in a quick smile.

Towering oaks surrounded most of their chosen campsite, interspersed by great rocks coated in a mossy fabric. One sheer rock face was almost as tall as their house and red paint hid beneath draping vines and ivy. Even out here in the middle of the countryside you can't escape graffiti. The path they had followed—if they could truly call it that—cut back into the woods and towards the quaint village of Mabley Holt.

He hefted his own rucksack free and propped it against one of the many rocks that dotted the clearing. Like nature's furniture some were as large as chairs, and no doubt the smaller ones would be used as such.

Kirsty crouched beside her bag. "I'll get the tent up, you work out where you want your fire."

"My fire?"

"Yeah, you love doing the caveman thing."

He couldn't disagree. The past year while saving for the wedding, their holidays were all about camping. He loved it, so did she. No air pollution, no light pollution. And as for the campfires, they connected with him on some primordial level. Somewhere deep within us all is that caveman who first discovered fire.

A small indentation in the grass would make the perfect fire pit, and some of the rocks shouldn't be too difficult to shift into position. He strolled towards the nearest. Similar to the rock face, red paint coated its surface. Pete clawed away some moss. Despite the sun burning his neck, the rock was cold and moist, almost sweaty.

"That'd make a great tattoo." Kirsty's voice came from over his shoulder. She held a couple of tent pegs.

"My next one?" He scraped away more moss and traced a finger along the contours of the faded paint: dark red, like a cave painting no less, of an unfamiliar symbol of triangles and curves.

"It's cool."

"It's peculiar," he said and picked moss from beneath his fingernail.

She nodded.

He shuffled to another rock. "Looks like they're all covered with similar markings." He counted six in total, seven if you included the larger symbol on the rock face. Some were of circles and lines, others with triangles and arcs. He'd never before seen anything like it.

"Weird." She turned away and knocked the pegs together. They chimed in a muted, dead kind of way. "Shame you can't take a picture."

"No tech."

It had been his idea to hike this far out into the countryside, and Kirsty had immediately suggested leaving technology at home. Phones as well. They'd even joked about how a cigarette lighter was hi-tech compared to a box of matches, so made sure to bring only the kitchen matches. The gas lantern he'd grabbed off his parents was his favourite old-school gadget, even though it was bulky.

He dragged his bag away from the rocks ready to shift them when Kirsty began coughing, then choking. He lurched upright and dropped the bag. It fell sideways into the long grass.

Doubled-over, she clutched her chest and spat. Sacks of burst fungi streaked the grass like torn cloth. Black clumps covered her boots and peppered her jeans. Spores drifted in a dark cloud.

She coughed again and straightened up, her face twisted in a comical grimace.

"You okay?" he asked.

She dragged the back of a hand across her lips. "Tastes like crap."

With the sun much lower, cold shadows had crept across the clearing and swallowed their tent. In the sunshine it was still hot but underneath the looming rocks Pete was reminded that it was, after all, only spring. They had a lot more camping trips to look forward to come summer.

He sat on a rock in front of the unlit campfire. It was his favourite rock. After erecting the tent and stowing away their supplies, he'd circled the clearing and removed all the moss from the rocks, satisfying himself in revealing each symbol in its entirety. As he'd shifted a couple to place around the fire pit, one—long and thin—broke in half. Kirsty had laughed and called him an idiot. She didn't see the point in moving them.

"Can't make a fire pit without rocks surrounding it," he'd told her.

Now, beside him, Kirsty coughed.

He looked at her. "You feeling any better?"

Her eyes watered. "Yeah."

"I've been thinking," he said, "about that teenager."

"What teenager?"

"The one on the doorstep of the village shop. With his skateboard and muddy feet."

"I'd forgotten about him." She rubbed her forehead and frowned.

Pete pulled the box of matches out of his pocket. "He was a pyromaniac."

She laughed but it sounded strained. "Yeah, he was."

Pete recalled the smell of burning plastic as that kid sat there, dressed in black shorts and a red T-shirt, holding a Zippo lighter to an action figure. He'd been melting the arms from one figure onto the other. Both were such a mess it was impossible to determine which franchise they belonged to.

Kirsty coughed again.

"Time for the fire," Pete said and crouched.

"You've been waiting—" another cough "—all afternoon for this moment."

He struck a match and held it to the kindling. Flames curled and smoke drifted. He lowered his face nearer the ground and gently blew. The fire crackled and spread further around the base of the pyre.

When he looked up, Kirsty's jaw was slack. Her gaze unfocused, gormless.

He laughed, then caught himself. "Kirsty?"

No response.

"Kirsty?"

Silence. Even the pre-dusk birdsong had quietened.

"Kirsty!"

Pete then spent what felt like the rest of the evening shaking her. Eventually his desperation became face slaps; gentle at first, then harder.

Dusk came, went, and something in the woods creaked, cracked and…

Splinters of trunk tore up the earth and a tangle of branches crushed the tent. Leaves whipped up into the night. Pete scrambled to his feet and almost fell into the campfire while Kirsty remained hunched on a rock, her eyes still fixed on middle-distance. Silent, unresponsive.

And now a great oak had flattened their tent.

The night pressed down. His hands clawed his head, tugged at his hat. "No!"

Silence.

He circled the campfire, again almost tripped, and ran towards the tent now hidden by the fallen oak. He dropped to a crouch. Resistant branches stabbed him as he scrambled on hands and knees. Leaves slapped him and twigs scratched his face. Squinting, the fire offering little light, he untangled the guy ropes. Some still fixed into the ground, others were missing. Finally, he reached the twisted canvas. The fabric was torn, pinned down by the tree.

Almost all their supplies and equipment were in the tent. He and Kirsty were lucky they'd not been in there, too. How had this happened? There was hardly any wind, especially with the surrounding rocks.

Cradled in the arms of that bastard tree, Pete lowered his head and closed his eyes. This whole trip had turned into a nightmare. His breath hissed between pursed lips, and his heart thumped at his temples. Remaining on hands and knees, he backed away from the tent they'd never get to sleep in. A stone bit into his kneecap. He grunted, clenched his teeth, and kept going.

Eventually, he pulled himself free and once again sat beside Kirsty on the cold rock.

What the hell was wrong with her? As earlier when she fell unresponsive, he considered finding the nearest house. If not a house, then perhaps he could return to the village. Their hike to this area had been long and he doubted anything would be open by the time he got there. Though you never knew with these sleepy rural villages; those ye olde-type pubs may pull all-nighters. In fact, he doubted if they'd even seen a pub on their hike. As far as he could remember, there was a dilapidated general store and little else.

But he would not leave her.

Through hair that clumped her forehead, her face glowed orange from the campfire. He placed a hand on her shoulder, squeezed, and let go. After slapping her, he'd given up expecting response and even now it was as though he felt his palm tingle from where he'd hit her. He hated himself for that. He hated all of this.

He stuffed a hand into her coat pocket, hoping, hoping…and found the house keys. His fingers curled around a pencil-torch. They rattled as he tugged them free, and after detaching the torch, he replaced them.

"No tech," he said to her as he twisted it.

The beam, thin, tiny, poked the darkness. The shadows refused to retreat. He circled the fallen tree, ducked beneath a splintered branch and once more headed for the tent. His scurry proved as difficult as the other side, however a little more of the tent was accessible. With the torch clamped between his teeth, he pulled out his penknife—thank God that hadn't been in the tent. He sliced the fabric, ripped it wider and plunged an arm in. Left, right, further forward, and he felt the sleeping bag, tugged it. He kept pulling and the whole thing whistled as the surrounding branches stroked it. Rummaging blindly again, his fingers prodded something soft. It moved. He grabbed it... A loaf of bread. Seconds passed, blindly flailing, desperate; nothing else to salvage. Not even the lantern. At least they now had food. Plus there was a bottle of water over by the campfire. Ramming the bread in the sleeping bag, he wriggled out through tangled branches. The sleeping bag snaked behind him on his way back to Kirsty. It even hissed through the grass.

He slid the torch into a pocket. "Got food."

The loaf he placed at her feet, and the sleeping bag he wrapped around her legs, over her arms. He sat beside her on another rock, the jagged surface biting into his arse.

The wind caught the fire and threw smoke his way. He coughed.

Earlier, as they'd trekked through the countryside, a burnt smell stole the fresh air. Having rounded a copse, the ruins of a manor house squatted blackened on the distant landscape. The sunshine and the spring colours potent enough to sharpen the scene. Even from that distance, they saw police tape flapping on the wind. Piles of charred masonry heaped in the surrounding gardens. Sunlight glinted from shattered panes and what may have been a car wreck or two.

Kirsty had said, "Bet that was an impressive inferno."

Pete now stared into their dying campfire; no more logs to hand. Shadows teased the surrounding rocks and made the strange markings dance. He reached out, saw his hand shake, and squeezed Kirsty's thigh through the sleeping bag. With his other hand, he raked fingers through his stubble. He eyed the fallen oak. What a mess.

He stood, torch spearing its pathetic beam into the woods, and went in search of more logs. Out from the circle of warmth, immediately a chill drove through his clothes.

Twigs snapped beneath each footfall and he came to a rocky ledge overlooking a slope. It was a kind of basin, maybe even a bomb crater, now cupping only rocks and trees. From the rim, the fallen tree cleaved rocks in two and spread its devastation behind him, out into their campsite.

The light flickered, went out.

Darkness swallowed him.

He shook the torch then slapped it in his palm. Popping the battery compartment free in a sticky mess, a sweet metallic smell burned his nostrils. The battery fell out and landed with a rustle of leaves.

"Ridiculous," he whispered into the dark and stuffed the useless thing into a pocket.

His feet stiffened. The knowledge of a short fall somewhere near fired iron rods up his legs. His stomach somersaulted. Looking up, he spied moonlight through the ceiling of branches. He didn't need the torch, already his eyes were becoming accustomed to the gloom. He backed away from the slope.

A foot slid sideways.

His arse landed on a tree root. Pain shot up his back. The basin—the *crater*—yawned wide. One hand slid in something wet, sloppy. At first he thought it was mud but in the faint light he saw a rotten log. Millipedes and beetles seethed. He yanked out his hand in a spray of insects.

He shivered and kicked out. The crater widened and gaped, darker, and he jerked and smacked his head on something behind him. Colours flashed across his vision. The darkness reached up and out to grab his stomach. One hand clamped the fence post he'd banged his head on. Rusted barbed wire tore into his palm. He winced.

That vertiginous tug ceased. Finally.

His heart pulsed in his throat, and he stood. Earth and leaves and sticks fell from his clothes, stones clattered into the crater. Pain throbbed from where he'd landed, and the cut on his palm stung. He scowled at the hollow log and the mass of insects.

He couldn't return to camp without fuel for the fire and so with extra care, he collected as much dry wood as he could carry and headed back. His body ached with every step. Like a beacon in fog, the campfire beckoned through the trees. The glow barely lit Kirsty's lowered head. Hair draped across her blank stare.

He stacked most of the wood beside the fire, saving two small logs to drop onto the embers. In seconds tiny flames flickered and curled.

"You'll be alright in the morning," he said to Kirsty.

Her lips parted, her head shot back, then forward, and she shouted what sounded like, "Turn them off!"

She slipped sideways, away from him. Her head smacked the ground inches from a small rock—one with what looked like the number eight painted on it.

Pete scrambled towards her and snatched the rock away. "Kirsty?" he whispered from a dry throat. "Kirsty, talk to me."

"Turlamov," she murmured. Her eyes showed little of the whites. Dark, impenetrable.

He wiped hair from her damp brow. What did that mean, *Turlamov*?

Kirsty's eyes looked like that of a drug addict. Indeed, it was more than that, they reminded him of something else, *someone* else. He didn't know who…and then it came to him: the teenager they'd seen in the village. The kid who'd sat on the doorstep burning stuff with a Zippo, bare-footed and with mud-caked clothes.

Pete reached for the loaf of bread. Opening it, his fingers sank into something sticky. Sweet, putrid. He coughed as the stink shot up his nostrils. He threw it behind him and he heard it land against the rock with a wet slap.

How could that even happen? It had been fresh when they'd bought it.

The only thing they now had beside his penknife and a torch without batteries, was the water bottle cradled between a couple of rocks. The flames reflected in the plastic. He grabbed it and unscrewed the lid. Kirsty still laid on her side but he managed to hold the bottle to her lips. She drank some, even licked her lips—finally some response.

She swallowed and said, "Thank you."

Those words, those two ordinary words heard every day, filled him with hope. He brought the bottle of water to his own lips and guzzled.

And spat it out into the campfire. The flames hissed.

Bitter water dribbled down his chin and he wiped it with the back of a hand. He spat again and tossed the bottle aside. It sloshed and inverted, and gushed into the tall grass.

He wrapped the sleeping bag tighter around Kirsty. Drinking the foul water couldn't be any worse than inhaling those spores. She now looked as though she slept, peaceful and huddled against a larger rock. He'd leave her for the moment, see what she was like in an hour or so. He could still taste the bitterness. How had the water turned like that? What with the mouldy bread, too… He eyed Kirsty, then the fallen oak. Pushing himself to his feet, he stretched. There was no way he could sleep.

At the edge of the clearing, black shapes hid in the grass alongside rotten fence posts. More of those damn shrooms. Knowing they'd caused Kirsty's catatonic stupor, he made certain not to tread on them. He headed to the fallen oak. Following its length back into the woods, he saw how it cleaved the rocks. A lance of moonlight silvered the rock and there, hidden beneath years of moss growth, were more red markings similar to those in the clearing.

At the base of the felled tree, amid the heaved earth, roots twisted with great rusted hoops. Chain-links as thick as his arm and as large as a dinner plate. Pete reached out, curling his fingers around one. Although the mud was cool, the metal itself was warm. Hot, in fact…

Voices drifted towards him. From the campfire. Was Kirsty calling for him? He let go of the chain-link.

There were two voices. Someone was there that could help them…

He jogged back to camp.

Kirsty was sitting upright and looking up at someone. It was the teenager. He wore the same T-shirt and shorts he had earlier, and still was without footwear. Behind him, his skateboard leaned against the rock face where his shadow jittered. The fire was much larger now and Pete assumed the kid had placed the remaining logs on it—Kirsty probably hadn't, although she looked lucid enough. Through hair that clumped across her face, her eyes were still dark and almost sunken in their sockets.

Pete approached. All he heard was his own breath.

The teenager held the plastic mess he'd created when they first saw him. It had four arms, two legs, and a molten lump of a head.

Pete stood before them. Thoughts tumbled through his head.

When the kid spoke, his lips barely moved. "Time's up," he said. Fire reflected in his dark eyes. They were like black marbles. He held high his modified toy, then hurled it into the fire. Flames roared.

"What—" The stink snatched Pete's voice and he coughed.

The kid's toes dug into the earth.

"Kirsty?" Pete knelt in front of her.

She said nothing.

From behind him in the woods, something cracked and echoed.

The earth shook and Pete almost fell as he turned. An earthquake? In the south-east of England? He knew these things happened occasionally, but... He glanced at the fallen tree. Had there been another one earlier?

Something in the woods snapped and crashed.

More rumbles. And the clattering, splitting sound of tumbling rocks made him wince. He had to get out of there. And what the hell was the kid doing here?

A wind pushed into the clearing and Pete squinted into its bite.

"We gotta go!" he yelled at Kirsty. His forehead hurt from where he frowned so hard. Although the fire roared inside a smoky whorl, a darkness closed in. Cloying, reaching through the trees, over the rock face, and into the clearing. The moon slid behind something more than clouds.

The wind buffeted him, and the fire hissed and spat in a cascade of leaves and dirt and stones. The taste of grit was bitter on his tongue.

From beside him someone shrieked. Muffled, strangled.

Pete turned.

The teenager was hunched, head down. It looked as though he'd somehow shrunk. His T-shirt and shorts now clung to his stick-like frame, his knees and elbows twisted at awkward angles. Buckled in some way, deformed. The kid's head jerked up. No face... The scalp was little more than patches of dark hair yet his face was as smooth and featureless as a pink balloon. No. Face. Flesh taut, glistening, and dark traceries of veins squirmed beneath the surface, bulging, wriggling.

Pete yelled and stepped back nearer the campfire. One side of his face itched from the heat and his heart filled his throat, bile rising.

Kirsty's voice drifted through the fuzziness in his head. "Pete?"

With such effort, he turned.

Her eyes focused, no longer sunken black orbs—was she finally lucid? There was, however, a black goo dribbling over her lips.

"Come on!" he shouted. The taste of smoke clawed his throat.

She looked up, over his shoulder, and she screamed.

Something shoved him from behind and his head snapped back. His legs tangled in the sleeping bag. He shot forward and landed near the fire, the heat intense. Dizziness came at him in waves. Through blurred vision, he saw Kirsty on her back, the creature on her chest, her head clamped between gnarly fingers. Her arms twitched.

Pete scrambled up, unsteady.

The creature leaned over her, its head—that faceless head—rubbed against her lips. Black goo smeared her cheek.

Pete grabbed a rock. Agony flared up his arm and he almost dropped it. Hot.

He smacked the rock into the creature's head.

Its spindly limbs flailed as it fell from Kirsty and thumped the ground. A tar-like substance pumped from the dented mess of its skull. Ruptured veins like purple spaghetti flopped and squirmed. An arm twitched once, twice, and the legs kicked. Then the creature was still.

Pete's hand burned and he dropped the rock. Black stuff splashed as it bounced and rolled.

Massaging his palm, he crouched beside Kirsty.

Her eyelids fluttered.

"Kirsty?"

She groaned and tilted her head. "What—"

Pete's stomach churned and his shoulders slumped. Relief.

He wiped away the black muck on her face. It was sticky. "You okay?"

She nodded.

His hand stung and throbbed. His skin had blistered...marked, indeed *branded*, in the shape of one of the symbols: two triangles, one hollow, the other solid, with facing apexes and separated by a curved X. He squinted at it. It kind of looked like an hourglass.

Kirsty pushed herself up on one elbow, hair covering half her face. Her bottom lip quivered. But she was looking past him, across the clearing.

A darkness roiled and twisted in the woods, thickening the gloom. Barbed wire sprung from the already broken fence posts and lashed the air. Staples pinged off the rocks.

Needle-like pain lanced Pete's forehead and he wiped his brow. His hand came away slick.

Smoke billowed, shadows churned like dancing phantoms. Coils of wire whipped branches, leaves rushed with the wind. Darkness clotted the edge of the clearing; looming, shimmering as though Pete gaped at a pool of gravity-defying oil swelling against glass. The wire spiralled and wrapped around the darkness, seeming to pull it in. Into the form of a man taller than the trees. A torso, yes, with legs and arms—*four* arms—gangly yet muscular. Its head stretched impossibly long and wide and sported jagged horns. Like a silhouette against the churning smoke, this entity had no visible features. It was pure darkness. Its legs moved, as did its arms, giving the impression of walking or even marching. Yet it failed to advance, unable to pass through the smoke and shadows that tumbled over its shoulders and looped around its limbs. This thing was attempting to break into this world, onto their plane of existence.

Pete forced himself to breathe. It was as if the height of this thing created a sense of vertigo, only reversed and pushing down on him. His feet felt heavy, his whole body pressed into the earth.

He scanned the clearing.

The rocks that peppered the grass and also the ones surrounding the now-dying campfire glowed red. Not on fire, but with some inner light or energy.

What the hell? And that was just it; Hell was precisely where this four-armed Being came from. A demon.

The rocks, even the broken ones, pulsed. He thought of the chain-links in the oak tree's roots. Before he and Kirsty disturbed the area, had a chain somehow contained the demon? On its own perhaps not, so in addition the symbols completed this ancient prison.

Or at least they had.

Smoke scratched his eyes and he rubbed them. His hand was cooling now, yet still the flesh was raw, angry. The barbed-wire cut had healed, leaving a jagged and fresh scar in line with the hourglass pattern.

"Pete." Kirsty's voice drifted towards him.

He stood. Hand raised before him, palm forward, he turned. His splayed fingers blocked the view of the demon but he knew it was there, seething in the darkness and close, so close to entering this world. His hand, his whole arm, tingled and warmed. A red light flared and shot from his fingers. From the rocks too, the same blinding light zigzagged to connect every symbol, every rock. Fire, yes, but a fire that didn't burn—at least, it failed to burn Pete. Just warmth; a comforting, soothing heat. The clean smell of ozone came with it. Red beams turned orange, into yellow and white. Incredible energy, bright, dazzling. The whole clearing lit up as though a midday sun had returned.

The darkness cracked like a stone-chipped windscreen.

A roar of defiance echoed.

Pete heard Kirsty shuffle backwards. He straightened his legs, dug his heels into the grass, as the rush of energy pushed against him.

The shadows ripped like fabric. Shredded and diminished. Smaller, smaller.

Light faded and Pete no longer had to squint. His jaw ached from where he clenched his teeth.

The demon's silhouette faded into the remaining wisps of torn shadow, now just a ghost cradled in grey swirls in what reminded Pete of curdled milk.

The trees shivered as though they relaxed, and the wind lessened and smoke drifted. Shadows, normal shadows, remained. The light emanating from the rocks further faded and the clearing dimmed. Moonlight returned. White, pure. Clean.

Silence.

He circled the dying campfire and headed for the teenager's body. The mutated head still oozed black filth but the veins no longer squirmed. A spindly arm lay beside it, and that's what Pete stared at.

Kirsty came up behind him, her breath hot at his collar as she hugged him. "What does it mean?" She sounded close to tears.

He clutched his stinging hand to his chest. The symbol was still there in his palm and blended with the barbed-wire wound. No longer raw; now lumpy and red like a scar. Like a tattoo. Somehow he knew it to be the demon's symbol, indeed a *sigil*.

It was also branded on the inside of the kid's forearm.

Pete knew he'd be learning much more about this entity. And he had absolutely no choice in the matter.

WELCOME HOME

The branch had punched through the windscreen and speared Tracy into the seat. Hopes of finding her friend, Amanda, now lay shattered with the glass in her lap.

No pain, just warmth. Even her heartbeat's thunder had diluted into the silence. All she felt was the blood pumping from her chest, drenching her clothes. Her hands failed to respond, her legs just as dead. It was as though it was Death's hand that had snatched the car from the road and slammed it into the tree.

Manic thoughts crashed into her head as her vision darkened. She cared little for the blood that gushed around the branch, nor did she now care how useless the Greek police had been. A day—or was it two?—had passed since Amanda vanished. The police didn't seem concerned. And now she'd had an accident. She wouldn't be able to afford the insurance on this rental car. Where was Amanda? She'd vanished last night...or was it last week? The police...couldn't help. The branch...all this blood. Where was she? They were supposed to fly home today.

Her vision flashed in a patchwork of light and darkness, and somewhere amid those trailing shadows came the swoop of black wings. A moth, floating in a gloom she assumed to be night's approach. Its legs thumped the dashboard. Each leg didn't just titter, they *crashed* into the plastic, stinging her ears. Sharp, penetrating. She winced.

The moth skittered closer—the thing had to be at least the size of her hand. With antennae twitching, its proboscis swayed and reached out. A black goo dripped from the end and blistered the dashboard. A curl of smoke drifted upwards, the smouldering stink burning her nostrils. This winged creature leapt towards her, clutching at her face. Pinching, scratching…and the proboscis stabbed her skin. A needle of agony. In. Out. In and out. In-out-in-out-in-out. In.

A fire raged beneath her flesh.

Out, and in again.

Shadows clogged her periphery, this time more a liquid darkness rather than the promise of night. Her heart smashed against her ribcage and her stomach churned. She coughed and blood spattered the steering wheel.

In-out-in-out.

In.

Out… In.

The moth detached itself, wings whipping the air as it hovered near the shattered windscreen.

And the flames raged through her every pore, spreading, sinking deeper, seething upwards, downwards, filling her body. An energy pulsed and slammed where her heart thrashed out its final rush of life.

Silence and darkness; a quiet nothingness.

Her fingers twitched. Heat raced through her veins, the darkness powering fluttery movements. Her muscles flexed. Life? Her arms jittered and rose higher, and one at a time her fingers gripped the branch. This *un*-life surged. She squeezed and the bark split beneath her fingers. Her nails splintered with the wood. She yanked the branch from her chest. Slurp. Gush. Blood—and darkness—spewed from her torso. Glass cracked and metal wrenched; the sounds shrill to her ears.

She tore off her seat belt, shredding the fabric, and kicked the door. Metal screeched. It echoed through the woods.

Charged with this fierce energy, she clambered from the wreckage, her life force drained…now replaced by a welcome blackness.

The moth drifted with the shadows, just ahead. Tendrils of that peculiar darkness teased its abdomen, seeming to beckon her, taunt her, promising an existence beneath the veneer of her past life. Beneath…

Shadowy curls toyed with its antennae, and on its thorax she saw a reflection of Death's grin.

Tracy followed the winged creature into the welcoming folds of shadow.

The smell was worse. Last time, the body was only two hours' dead; this time it was two days. Such a difference. For a moment, Amanda wondered how many more bodies she'd find before the shadows allowed her peace.

She pushed a rag to her face, coughing. With her other hand she swatted the flies. Her bare feet sank into the sand, suggesting the tide was coming in. As the only human on the island, she was there to obey, and if she fought that peculiar obedience, the shadows—her puppeteers—made her do things, made her think things. Vile things no lady should ever think, let alone action. These last several days, all she was ever with was Death. She'd be just another body soon, she knew that. Dead, and then fuel for the shadows.

With reluctance, she poked the rag beneath her bikini waistband and grabbed the corpse by its feet. Grunting, grimacing, she heaved it towards the tree line. Her strength amazed her. This was one fat Greek; bloated, the flesh shrivelled by the sun and the sea. His head left a snake of disturbed sand behind. Maybe she recognised him from the main island. Perhaps, last week, he'd served her and Tracy cocktails.

Tracy?

A flood of grey pushed into Amanda's head and the memories tumbled away as though the shadows snatched thoughts of her friend, their holiday, of everything.

Now almost out of the sunlight, her muscles screaming, she closed her eyes. She hated to come in from the sun, yet she did it. Obeying the shadows was all that mattered. Still with her eyes closed, she felt the shade wrap around her, and she dropped the Greek's legs. The sound—that dead sound—echoed through the trees. Scratching her neck, fingers raking sunburn, her nerves flared as though a blowtorch seared the skin. Another waft of the wet salty stink, and she spewed. At least the shadows allowed her that much. When she'd finished, she wiped her mouth.

"Let the shadows take me," she whispered, finally opening her eyes. The bitterness still inside, her legs folded and she sat cross-legged. She squinted into sunlight that lanced through branches, a broken canopy offering little reassurance from the clogging shadows in her peripheral vision.

How many other islands like this existed in the Mediterranean? A place of solitude for the solo-traveller, a romantic escape for others, or a break for best friends…again memories collided, jagged images of…Tracy. Where was Tracy?

Amanda's breath came short and sharp, her eyes darting left and right. What was all this? When were they supposed to be going home?

The island.

That's what was important. This island where the shadows own you, where the shadows feed on the bodies they find. That same darkness kept Amanda alive, only just, to drag corpses from the sunlight, to bring them to the centre of the island. To the Temple.

Her past no longer mattered. She knew her body would soon be offered. Often, those playful shadows suggested that.

She wished it would be now.

She was ready.

Further ahead, the grinding of stone over stone made her blink into the unfolding darkness. Close to where ancient rock huddled in the embrace of grey vines, the darkness thickened. It rippled and seethed, somehow energised.

A cloud of flitting shadow burst from its heart, expanding outwards. This was something Amanda had never before witnessed. She frowned. This wasn't shadow, this was not that familiar darkness but a swarm of moths. Like black fog, wings too loud on the air, hundreds, *thousands*, of moths rushed towards her, up and into the trees.

She shrieked and ducked, but none came near. In seconds, they vanished into the surrounding darkness, into the deepening shadows. Several lingered, coming to rest on vine trunks and mossy stone.

Finally, she straightened.

From the remaining darkness, a woman emerged. Framed in shadow, vines, and crumbling stonework, her clothes glistened red, sodden.

Amanda's throat was dry. "Tracy?"

Her friend nodded and dark flecks shot from dripping hair.

"Where have you been?" Amanda asked.

"Here," said Tracy. She stretched out her arms. The shadows coiled around her hands, toying with broken fingernails.

Amanda walked forward. The shadows parted to allow her closer than she had ever been to those ancient stones.

"Welcome home," Tracy whispered as the two friends embraced.

The alarm thundered into Terry's skull, and he kicked at the darkness. His chest heaved. The duvet slid from his body and he squinted at the clock: 3.33 a.m. Again?

He punched it silent.

What the hell was this? He'd set the thing for six, and this was the third morning it'd happened. Only this time was different. A lance of moonlight pushed enough into the room for him to see his fist hanging over the edge of the bed. Poking between the knuckles was a piece of paper. Bringing it closer, his fingers uncurled and he recognised his handwriting: *Release the Forgotten.*

Beside him, Kate moaned into her pillow and yanked the covers. "What is it with that thing?"

Terry's heart smashed against his ribs, and he pulled back his arm. His fingers crushed the paper again. It sounded like a dead leaf.

"Give me it." Her face was squashed into the pillow.

"What?" His voice sounded pathetic.

A rigid finger speared over his head. "The clock."

She snatched it from him. Her fingers darted over its casing and she hooked off the back cover, shook out the battery and threw the clock over the side of the bed. Something cracked, and as she rolled over, the battery thumped to the floor.

Silence returned and Terry stared at the back of her head. He closed his eyes. How had he written something while sleeping? That was ridiculous.

Minutes passed and Kate's breathing became softer. Without much of the duvet over him, it was easy to slide out of bed. A floorboard groaned, and Terry prayed it didn't wake her. He listened for a response, but her breath stayed rhythmic.

He didn't need waking up, but he knew he needed coffee. He pulled on his dressing gown.

Downstairs, he went into the kitchen and the cold linoleum bit his feet. He loaded the percolator and it began its boil, making that sound of pebbles being dragged by the tide. He squinted through the kitchen window, through the pale reflection of his face. His disembodied head hovered over the recently-laid turf. Darkness swallowed the new shrubs, the trees, the patio and the expensive garden furniture Kate had insisted they bought. They still hadn't paid it off. Their debt was another reason for getting that promising work contract. He knew he should prepare for the presentation next week... but no. It could wait.

Mug in hand, he wandered into the garden. The chill darkness pressed in on him and he sat at the table. The lawn looked much better now they'd agreed to do something with it. Those rolls of new turf pushed neatly up to flowerbeds and shrubs, without a weed in sight. That shop-smell fragrance seemed dampened by the shadows. He had no idea what they'd planted, he simply let Kate choose whatever she wanted. She wanted more from him certainly, yet that was all he could do right now. She wanted children, a bigger house. And they needed more money for all of that. He knew it was a lame compromise and redoing the garden was a temporary fix, but she still made things awkward. Sometimes he felt he couldn't keep up with her demands.

Terry watched the shadows gradually retreat as the sun peered over the fence and bled into the trees. His coffee remained untouched.

His working day that followed was typical. Nothing unusual, apart from his constant rereading of the scribbled note. The last few nights of ruined sleep had stolen his focus, and he knew he was dangerously close to losing his job. A lot was riding on that one contract.

He needed more sleep.

All day, however, he thought of little else: *Release the Forgotten*. What did that mean? And why was it always 3.33 a.m.? During lunch he searched online for any symbolic reference to it. He'd never before been willing to accept such nonsense and believed all things to be reasonably justified, but this was getting ridiculous. It didn't take long for him to learn the hours around 3 a.m. were known as the Witching Hour, the Devil's Hour and sometimes even the Dead Hour. Bullshit, all of it.

He got home before Kate, and through the front door he booted his briefcase. It smacked the sofa.

The next half hour crawled by. Again, his thoughts were on the Forgotten, whoever they were. When Kate got in, her venom spat into the kitchen.

She still clutched her bag. "Where's dinner?"

This was all there was these days, no matter what he did. Recently he'd been waking up during the Dead Hour. To him, this was beginning to feel like a dead relationship. Maybe it was related.

Following his lack of response, they shared only necessary words as they prepared food between them. The evening was then spent with Kate glued to the TV while Terry's eyelids were glued shut. When he woke it was midnight, all lights off and Kate in bed. He guessed he should go and join her. He didn't want to.

The TV's red eye on standby stared from out of the darkness.

The alarm yanked him upright, his heart almost choking him. He jerked from bed, not even trying to keep quiet, eyeing Kate's silhouette. She didn't budge. How was that possible?

The clock. Where was it? He stamped on the battery, pain firing up his leg. Somehow he managed not to cry out.

The alarm still pierced the night.

He scrabbled across the floor and found it. Its glass had cracked and it said 3.33—of course. He squeezed the button and it silenced. The alarm echoed like a ghost. Fumbling with the stupid thing, he found the battery compartment empty. Somehow he knew it would be.

The red glow of digits faded.

Was he dreaming? When he grabbed his dressing gown the fabric felt real enough.

Once downstairs, he placed the clock on the coffee table. The next few hours drifted past as he thumbed the TV remote.

He left for work early, without breakfast, eyes as heavy as his briefcase. He didn't care for not having done any homework. At the office, cradling a sugarless coffee, he couldn't remember if he'd even said goodbye to Kate, or if she'd replied.

Terry's day was short. After telling his boss he was ill, the bastard sent him home with a stack of files. When he got in, he threw them beside the sofa and collapsed into it.

Kate's shouting wrenched him from sleep, his heart slamming into his throat.

"...This mess?" Her face was blotchy, her mouth twisted.

His tongue stuck to the roof of his mouth, and as he pushed himself upright he realised he held a marker pen. The lid was off and there was black ink on his shirt, and over his hands. He dropped it and it clattered on the floor.

"Terry." Kate's eyes shot around the lounge. "What have you done?"

He dragged a hand down his cheek, round to the back of his neck, and squeezed. "Don't remember..."

"What is wrong with you?" With her face ugly, she bounded from the room. Upstairs, the bathroom door slammed, its echoes dying through the house.

Terry's stomach churned.

In thick black strokes he'd written on the walls and doors, the dresser, the coffee table, and on the floor. Feeling tiny, he could just make out a pattern scrawled across the dining-room table. Everywhere, barely legible in places, the words shared a similar urgency: *Release. Save. Forgotten.* On the front door, around the letterbox, it looked like he'd scrawled *switchblade*.

Why the hell would he write that? His head throbbed, the blood thrashing in his ears. He leaned back, the sofa swallowing him. He'd even written *Forgotten* on the ceiling.

A darkness leaked into his periphery, framing that word, and the ceiling pushed down on him. He sat upright, bent forward, and stared at his feet. From above, Kate's stomping lowered the ceiling further. What was happening to him?

Grabbing the pen, he hurled it at the TV—across its screen were the words, *Must save.*

He charged into the kitchen, clawed for the sink, and threw up.

Again the clock snatched a dreamless sleep from him. He fumbled for it. Yes, 3.33. It was on his bedside cabinet, and he didn't remember replacing it. He doubted Kate would've moved it. After getting in from work, and going mental at him for scribbling crap around the house, she'd left for the pub. He still couldn't believe her response; she hadn't even suggested a doctor's visit. Clearly he needed help. So no, she wouldn't have done anything so thoughtful. Certainly not after having returned home pissed and argumentative. She'd been doing that a lot recently, and he often found her with a glass of wine in hand.

From beside him, a grunt burst from her throat.

With those digits fading, he thought of the previous evening alone. He'd tried to start on the work files, but all he ended up doing was staring at his black hands. He knew he should've scrubbed the writing off everything as well, not just his hands. The only scribble he did remove was the one on the TV screen.

Kate's breath was ragged and she turned away. Things had been getting tough for them, certainly, and he suspected this was their end. He needed her now, more than ever, yet she was proving to be the unsupportive bitch she'd always been. The stink of cigarettes and alcohol clung to her. He wrinkled his nose. This was hell.

Squeezing his eyes shut, he wanted to scream and he didn't care if it woke up the neighbours.

Release…

Terry's eyes shot wide, and he squinted into the gloom. Had Kate whispered that?

We are here.

He glanced at her, ears straining. His heart pulsed in his throat. It wasn't her voice. Was there someone else in the room?

Release us…

It was in his head. Behind the surging of blood through his veins, a collection of voices rushed in. It was as if each whisper had substance, coiling tentacles around his brain. A cacophony of incomprehensible shouting.

He clamped hands over his ears, making no difference.

A voice roared above the others: *Help.*

Another screamed: *Find us.*

Others collectively yelled: *The blade.*

Black spots dotted his vision and he blinked, still clamping his head with slick palms. His breath felt as if every lungful was polluted with glass.

The crowd quietened.

The Witchblade, a few voices whispered. These were closer. What were they talking about?

Find the blade, they said. *Find us…*

Why did he have to find it? Find them? How?

The Forgotten, was the last thing a fading voice said.

Shivering, the roar of blood filled his head. He stared at the ceiling feeling sunrise push away the shadows.

Kate snatched the milk carton from him and tipped it over her cereal, spilling some. He watched it creep across the table and become a dribble of white tears. Each one exploded on the patio.

"You're not going into work?" She stabbed the spoon into her bowl, splashing the back of her hand. She didn't wipe that, either. "If you lose your job I'm never gonna leave this town."

Terry rubbed his eyes. The mornings were getting colder, and he knew they'd not enjoy breakfast in the garden for much longer. And there was rain waiting in the clouds, he could feel it. "That all you care about?"

"Do you think your boss won't take into consideration your sick days?"

"I…" Terry pushed his bowl away. He wasn't hungry. "I'm sick."

"Grow some balls, you're acting like a child."

There it was again: the child reference. That's all she thought of these days, but what about him? What about this madness? "Last night—"

"I don't care." Kate dragged a newspaper towards her and shoved cereal into her mouth. Her machine-gun crunching filled the garden. It seemed to ricochet off the fence.

From beyond their wooden walls a car honked; the world now awake. It seemed far away. He'd not eaten much of his cereal and as the silence closed in and pushed the world even further away, the milk soured on his tongue. Kate's chair scraped stone, and she rose. Still her jaw moved as she ground down on her mouthful. He followed her indoors.

She stopped beside the dining-room table and her fist pressed into the wood.

"Last night," Terry mumbled, "I heard… I don't know."

"I heard that alarm." Her eyes focused not on him, but the black scrawls over the table. "Again."

"Kate." He realised his voice cracked, and he straightened his back. This was ridiculous. He bit his lip. "I'm scared."

The pattern on the table was a series of circles and lines, reminding him of some devil-worshipping crap he'd seen somewhere. Again, he thought of what he'd read about the Devil's Hour and the connection with the voices. *Find the blade*, they'd said. Kate's fingernail traced a black curve. "I'm leaving," she said.

"What?" He stepped back and knocked the door. It smacked the wall and a shelf rattled.

"For good." Her eyes reflected the morning sunlight, and little else.

"Kate!"

Find us… He couldn't tell if the voice was in his head again or it was a stab of memory. He gaped as she marched into the lounge. She kicked his work folders, grabbed her bag and left.

The front door slammed with a dead echo.

He stared at the word *switchblade* on the back of the door. Then he noticed the S and W were almost one squiggle. It didn't say switchblade.

"Witchblade?" Terry's voice didn't sound like his own. *The blade*, they'd said, *find the blade, save the Forgotten.*

For the remainder of the day he mostly watched TV—or at least thumbed through the hundreds of channels it offered. He didn't eat. Occasionally his mobile would ring. It was his boss, and Terry imagined the bastard's scowl. He never answered it, and soon turned it off. The landline also rang several times. Eventually he yanked the wire from the wall, the plaster crumbling.

Sometime during the afternoon he sat in the garden and he stared at the new turf. The joins between the rolls were fading. He remembered how the garden had been a barren stretch of weeds, where in the centre a curious formation of mushrooms had taken over. It was a hulk of grey and black fungi, their caps as wide as his hand with stalks that seemed to sweat. That lot took a surprising effort to destroy. They had exploded in black puffs, and he fancied he could still taste those spores. That heavy, earthy scent had lingered at the back of his throat for days.

Rain soon forced him indoors and the chaos pressed in. He sat on the sofa. At his feet were the work folders, a bleached rainbow of what his life represented. Scattered, forgotten. One sported a scribble: *Use the Witchblade.* He knew he should remove those scrawls, try to return sanity to his life. Everywhere he looked, apart from the TV, something reminded him of the madness. And that was just it, maybe he was going mad. No, there was no maybe about it. This was the onset of insanity. The voices proved that. *The Forgotten...*

He couldn't give a shit about the Forgotten, he wanted to forget.

With the TV volume down, he sank into the sofa and closed his eyes. Sleep soon came. As always, dreamless.

This time the alarm didn't wake him, it was the moment the shovel he held jarred on something metal. Its clang muted, dead. His brain flooded like the ground beneath his bare feet. His vision sharpened and he squinted into the darkness.

Freezing clothes hugged him. He stood in the middle of the garden, over a gaping hole. Rain filled it, churning with grass and leaves and clumps of earth. The new turf was peeled back and on top was the clock: 3.32. That last digit flicking to a three. There was no alarm. It remained on 3.33 for a second and then faded.

How did he get here? And why was he holding a shovel? He threw it down. It slapped the ground in a dirty spray. His legs buckled, and water rushed up and soaked him further. The mud sucked his arms, pulling him into the hole. Something raked his forearm.

From a constricted throat, he cried out.

Water sloshed as he struggled. His chest heaved, his jaw so tight his teeth hurt. Then he clasped something rough, metallic. He remembered the shovel jarring on metal. There was something angled, perhaps a box. The more he wiggled his fingers, the more the earth loosened. Clamping his hands around the object, he tugged, his back screaming.

He slipped and fell backwards, his prize dripping mud from above. He dropped it beside him and got to his knees. The air was cold in his lungs.

He scooped away the earth and located the hinges, then a clasp. He twisted it and it snapped. The hinges sheared off, cracking the night. Inside was a bunch of oily rags. The smell reminded him of that time, as a kid, he'd visited a farm: the greasy, cloying smell of old machinery and well-used tools. He pulled at the rags, but they came out as one heavy lump. They were stubborn as he unravelled them, and each slapped the ground and splashed him. No farm tools here.

With slippery hands he removed a knife. He wasn't surprised.

The Witchblade. This was it. Its hilt was an ornate knot, its blade curved and ending in a nasty point. It glinted in the moonlight. Possibly silver.

He staggered to his feet. His vision blurred, and spots of colour stabbed his periphery. He kicked the box and it splashed into the hole. With his mind reeling, a chill crept into his veins. It was as if the shadows began folding inwards. A darkness pressed in. Motionless, he gripped the Witchblade in numb fingers.

Find us…

His heart slammed in his head, knocking away the darkness that filled him. The ground sucked his feet as he paced backwards.

He soon made it into the house.

Save the Forgotten.

Walking up the stairs, he dragged the Witchblade along the wall, its tip shrieking as bits of paint fell away. His foot hovered above the next step and his eyes followed those chips as they dropped. It was as if he heard each crash, slamming into the carpet, filling the house like thunder.

He staggered into his study. The place was foreign, having not entered it for days. He dropped the Witchblade on top of a project file, and left the room. He knew he needed a bath… but didn't quite reach it.

He spent the day in and out of lucidity.

His eyelids fluttered and there was the Witchblade, reflecting lamplight. Its hilt gripped in white knuckles smeared red, just like the blade itself. It dripped on the bedroom carpet.

Why was he holding it?

There was Kate. In bed. Those red smears framed her body.

"Kate?" His voice sounded distant. When had she come back?

His stomach wrenched as Kate's unmoving body filled his vision. Shit. He'd killed her.

He crouched. More blood soaked his side of the bed. His heartbeat filled the room. It seemed to punch the walls.

Kate. Dead.

Sweat dripped from his forehead and with his free hand he wiped it, streaking blood—and mud—across his forearm.

"Kate..." He dropped the Witchblade on the bed and reached for her, his hand in slow motion, fingers like claws. A strange warmth flushed through him, yet there was a coldness there too.

Then Kate twitched and shifted position, murmuring. Where Terry leaned on the bed, his weight resisted her pull of the duvet and revealed her body: naked, clean.

No blood.

His breath snatched the air. Hot, cloying. Was she only sleeping? His eyes shot from Kate to the Witchblade, then to the surrounding blood, and back to Kate. Her hand tugged lazily at the duvet.

He eased himself up—such an effort—and watched her huddle beneath the bloodstained covers. The Witchblade shifted and he grabbed it. It was sticky.

Kate mumbled something.

She was alive. He'd not killed her.

A voice pushed into his confusion: *Release us.*

He saw the clock, sitting on his bedside table: 3.23 a.m. Not 3.33? He didn't question this for long.

The warmth leaked into a strange chill, and he looked down. He wore only trousers. His stomach was a raw mess, a torn eruption of what was once his abdomen. Blood oozed down his legs.

His head pulsed, spots dotting his vision. He managed to remain standing. He focused on his stomach, the red and purple stuff bulging between jagged flaps of skin.

Clenching the Witchblade in slick fingers, he knew this was self-inflicted. He shook his head. No pain, only that spreading chill.

He had to save the Forgotten.

With a hand that didn't look like his own, he reached for the clock: 3.24. Its battery compartment was empty, which no longer concerned him. There was still warmth in him, that's all that mattered.

He left Kate sleeping and walked downstairs. Each step deliberate, with the occasional creak snapping the air. The Witchblade steadied him, gouging the wall. His blood trickled over his toes, blending with muddy footprints.

At the bottom, the red digits announced 3.26.

In the lounge he trod on his work tie. It clung to his foot, and with each step it snaked behind him. He walked past the dining-room table, the pattern of circles and lines barely visible in the gloom.

Reaching the kitchen, he tucked the Witchblade in his belt. Now gripping the clock in both hands, it seemed to taunt him as the digits flickered to 3.28. Patterns of red streaked its casing.

The backdoor gaped like a black mouth and swallowed him as he stepped into the garden. The rain lanced his neck and pummelled the ground. The wind bullied the trees. His stomach was a flopping mess, and with his free hand he pushed his intestines back in. They bulged between splayed fingers.

The door swung to, and its creak stuttered into the night. A spear of light remained in the garden and did little to penetrate the stygian black that stretched beyond. He squinted at the contours of the patio furniture, the shrubs, the fence, the silhouette of trees against a looming sky. And the darkness closed in…

3.29.

Each step dragged. No pain as he headed for the shadows, towards the hole he'd dug the previous night. He walked around it, his tie still following like an obedient serpent.

3.30.

The darkness beckoned. His heart was a constant drumbeat.

His leg shot sideways and he dropped the clock. Both hands slapped the freezing mud. A bitterness peppered his lips and he spat. The accompanying crack of thunder was barely louder than his thrashing heart.

His face was near the clock: 3.31. Ahead, the shadows twisted, unfolded, releasing a swirl of faint colours. Like a diesel spill leaking into his garden the shadows edged towards him, a tsunami of darkness approaching.

Release us.

He pulled out the Witchblade, raising it, and slowly stood up. The blood thumping in his head slowed as if his heartbeat counted the seconds. He edged closer to the darkness, still with a hand pushed against his bulging abdomen. His other arm reached with the Witchblade. Closer. Closer.

The blade sliced the shadows like cut fabric.

Yesss.

He entered the void, his work tie still trailing.

3.32.

And inside he knew them. They were there, as glimmers of life forgotten.

No longer are we forgotten.

Their sparks of life force detached from the darkness within. Each started blinking out. The fewer there were, the colder he became. He almost felt their relief. It was like a teasing fire as winter burrowed into his soul.

As his life ebbed, so theirs moved on.

The shadows closed in, and Terry managed a final glance at his life. He saw the clock, its digits fading, reading 3.33.

THE SHADOW FABRIC

Novel extract

Unable to blink, I shot a quick glance around the dining room. My heartbeat stormed my head. I had to get out of there, I had to leave the other men to it. These brothers had a lot of hate to throw around.

The black fabric draped across the table and chair, tracing every contour. It flowed over the wood like liquid. Hugging tight whatever it touched, it turned everything into a shadow, a silhouette, a featureless dark blot of its former self. The way it moved defied physics.

My throat clamped around a cry that came out a whimper.

I had no idea what Stanley intended. The strange fabric didn't travel far from his hand, and where the material ended, it rippled and pulsed, pulling further away, yet unable to claim more of its surroundings. The more it unfolded, the dimmer the room became. My skin itched as it sapped the light.

Victor and Stanley stood facing each other: Victor, with his eyebrows pushed together, the ornate blade clenched in a fist, and Stanley, with his jaw tight and a twitch at the edge of his mouth. In Stanley's grasp the fabric quivered, its material reminding me of the way midday sunlight reflects from the surface of a swimming pool, the ripples a criss-crossing of movement. It was peaceful to behold, hypnotic almost. But this thing was dark and stifling to observe.

There was nothing remotely tranquil about this.

I wanted to leave them to whatever absurd game this was…yet my feet refused to move. The familiar ache in my knee rushed through my body, drumming in my skull, telling me I was useless. Since the car accident the knee often was useless. I couldn't leave Victor, I knew that. The man looked as terrified as I felt.

"I hate you, Victor." Stanley's nose was no more than a thumb's width from his brother's.

"No," Victor gasped. His hand shook, his knuckles whitening around the knife. "Don't!"

I didn't know who or what Victor spoke to. Was it Stanley? The shadows? The knife?

In a blur of darkness, shadows coiling his arm, the blade slammed into Stanley's chest. Blood spread and he staggered back.

Victor's eyes widened. Clutching the weapon, he stumbled from the fireplace, away from his brother. The knife slid out, sucking at the wound. A jet of scarlet misted the air, and then oozed.

I could only see darkness...so much darkness, and my lungs went tight.

The fabric—the Shadow Fabric—closed around Stanley's buckling legs.

The remaining material swept from the table, away from the violin case. Black tentacles whipped and grabbed Stanley. The darkness enfolded him as his eyes glazed over. It dragged his body along the carpet a short distance and tightened its grip.

My jaw muscles twitched as I clenched my teeth.

The Fabric began to shrink. Still in its embrace, the last I saw of Stanley was his dead stare.

"Vic..." I whispered, and gripped the back of the sofa.

My boss dragged his eyes away from the retreating shadows and stared at the knife. Behind him, the mantel clock hammered out several seconds before the weapon slipped from his hand onto the carpet, where it bounced with a red splash.

He fell to his knees. "Oh God."

The Fabric vanished.

I dashed across the room as much as my leg would allow and staggered to a halt beside him. Sobs wracked his frame as I grasped his bony shoulder.

On the table next to where Stanley had been standing was the violin case, still open like a crooked yawn.

A million thoughts tumbled through my head, but I couldn't find the words. I'd been Victor's chauffeur for no more than a day, and already I'd witnessed him stab his own brother. What the hell?

I don't know how long I remained like that, holding him, with light creeping reluctantly back into the room. Victor shouldn't have been surprised that the shadows had taken his brother. After all, those shadows—the darkness—are associated with all that is dead…or should be dead.

Silence clogged the air like we were buried in a tomb.

For some of us, there is a moment in our lives where all we've believed real is whipped out from under us and we're left to survive in a world that's a lie. All the things in life we've taken for granted are sheathed in a weak veneer, behind which stands the shadows.

For me, this was one of those moments.

ACKNOWLEDGEMENTS

While several stories in this collection have featured elsewhere in anthologies and ezines, some began as scraps of flash fiction. So if you recognise any thread then it is to you I send thanks—following your positive feedback and encouragement, you guys have pushed these stories forward. My gratitude also goes to Chris Shoebridge who is always on the end of a draft, whether the first scribbles or a final edit. And the largest thanks, I give to Helen. Without her this book would simply not exist.

ABOUT THE AUTHOR

Mark Cassell lives in a rural part of the UK with his wife and a number of animals. He often dreams of dystopian futures, peculiar creatures, and flitting shadows. Primarily a horror writer, his steampunk, dark fantasy, and SF stories have featured in several anthologies and ezines.

His popular SF universe, the Chaos Halo series featuring Alpha Beta Gamma Kill, can be found in the *Future Chronicles* ezine. Previously published episodes will be available as a collected works from Herbs House in 2016.

The short story collection, *Sinister Stitches*, is only a fraction of an expanding mythos that began with his debut novel, *The Shadow Fabric*, a supernatural horror tale of demons, devices, and deceit.

For more about Mark and his work, or to contact him directly:

Twitter: **@Mark_Cassell**

Facebook: **www.facebook.com/AuthorMarkCassell**

Blog: **www.beneath.co.uk**

Newsletter: **www.markcassell.com**

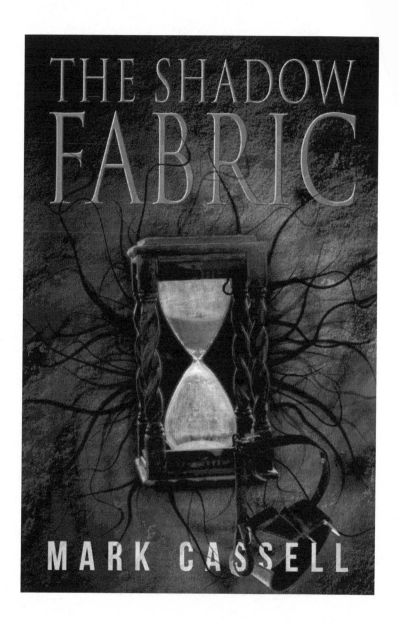

Available in paperback and digital from Herbs House

Made in the USA
Charleston, SC
12 July 2016